CELEBRITY VET

Veterinary nurse Tessa Dance takes on her live-in job in the New Forest with some trepidation. Her new employer is *the* Samuel Wilde, who is accustomed to female adoration, expects 'flexibility' from her — whatever that means — and who clearly anticipates Tessa falling at his feet too. She has to admit he is dangerously attractive, as well as a gifted veterinary surgeon, but trying to understand this complex man is surely playing with fire . . . ?

Books by Carol Wood
in the Linford Romance Library:

VET IN POWER

CAROL WOOD

CELEBRITY VET

Complete and Unabridged

LINFORD
Leicester

First published in Great Britain in 1993 by
Mills & Boon Limited
London

First Linford Edition
published 2013
by arrangement with
Mills & Boon Limited
London

A catalogue record for this book is available
from the British Library.

ISBN 978–1–4448–1687–7

Published by
F. A. Thorpe (Publishing)
Anstey, Leicestershire

Set by Words & Graphics Ltd.
Anstey, Leicestershire
Printed and bound in Great Britain by
T. J. International Ltd., Padstow, Cornwall

This book is printed on acid-free paper

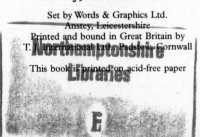

1

The second after opening her eyes, it all flooded back.

Why had she agreed to the interview, for goodness' sake?

Tessa stretched her long legs, throwing back the duvet. She must have had a brainstorm! A six a.m. start on a Saturday morning?

And the voice on the end of the line had been one of those lacklustre voices . . .

She should have thought of some excuse . . .

Perversely, two oval, deep green eyes began to open wide the moment she told herself she would remain in bed. A small but persistent fluttery feeling in the pit of her stomach now informed her she was missing the job of a lifetime.

Thrusting her bare feet into slippers,

she padded sleepily downstairs. A hazy May sun warmed the kitchen window-panes and three grey pigeons preened on the fence of the modern town-house garden.

Tessa peered at the birds through the pale curtain of fawn hair spilling heavily over her shoulders . . . and considered the three males in her life — and their reaction — if she told them she was leaving home.

But she wasn't leaving, not yet! She was only thinking about it!

Since her early teens she had looked after her twin brothers and her father. Surely, at twenty-three she could begin to plan out some sort of future for herself without feeling so guilty? After her mother's death it had seemed natural for her to slip into the maternal role, though in retrospect, with her born inclination to be bossy, the transition hadn't been too difficult.

But looking after Felix and Archie and her father had gone on just a shade too long, that was the trouble. The twins were hulking great men now — and they couldn't boil an egg between them! As for her father . . . he was only in his middle forties. She hated to see him putting all his energies into his building yard — what was to stop him remarrying again if she wasn't around?

Tessa blinked the sleepiness, and the problem of her family, from her eyes. For all her organisational skills, she hadn't managed to get any of them to give her a lift today. Not that she had asked. She could imagine their faces if she'd even begun to describe the job advertisement!

'Anyone home?'

Tessa swivelled to see the back door open, carelessly left unlocked by the last reveller home.

'Are you decent?' A male voice, accompanied by a hand clutching a wilting red rose, appeared at the door. 'Not that I mind if you're not — in fact, the last thing I'd object to is a little indecency first thing in the morning!'

Tessa's full mouth widened into a slow grin. 'You idiot, Todd — come in, for goodness' sake. But if it's indecency you're looking for, I suggest you go upstairs and take a look at Felix and Archie sleeping off their hangovers!'

'No, thanks!' Todd Greystone gave an appreciative leer at her skimpy nightwear, a baggy T-shirt with a Mickey Mouse motif. 'I don't fancy your brothers.' He grinned, the admiring blue eyes under a shock of white-blond hair sweeping their way over her.

Tessa threaded the flower into an empty milk bottle and reached over to place it on the windowsill. Turning back, she found Todd's gaze still fixed on her, his eyes flying up from her long bare legs. It was typical of her next-door neighbour to make an entrance like this. A physical fitness instructor at the local health farm, he liked to flaunt his developing physique. Growing up next door to the Greystones, Tessa remembered Todd as a gangling adolescent, but in the last few years nature had taken over his problems. Dressed in white shorts and a vest barely covering the broad, damp chest, he flexed his damp muscles, making her both stare and laugh at the same time.

'You should be more careful about drawing the blinds if you insist on walking around in that sort of gear,' he teased lightly. 'I had a ringside seat from over your fence.'

'Then you must have gone on tiptoe; that's a six-foot fence.'

'So? I'm six-one. Any complaints?'

She sighed in mock-exasperation. She had heard it all before from Felix and Archie. Their endless parade of woman-talk, bravado that worked just so long as a female didn't take them up on it.

'I've got more important things to worry about than Peeping Toms this morning!' She placed a firm hand on the hot chest, driving him backwards to the door.

'Such as!'

Tessa sighed again, this time seriously. 'If you really must know — a job interview, for which I am already late!'

'A bit early for an interview, isn't it?'

She looked up, her jade eyes still luminous from sleep. 'I have to be in a place called Beechwood Bridge, about two hours' drive from here. I've got to catch the six-thirty train.'

'You'll never make it!'

Tessa gritted her teeth. 'Thanks a lot! Very helpful!'

He grinned, precociously slipping an arm around her waist. She slapped him playfully and reluctantly he let her go. 'Spoilsport. I promise my intentions are purely honourable!'

'I'd never believe a promise of yours, Todd Greystone, not in a thousand years!'

'What if I promised to get you to your interview on time?'

'You wouldn't . . . would you?'

He laughed at her. 'I'll be back in twenty minutes — so don't keep me waiting!'

Tessa spent the next quarter of an hour in a mild frenzy, relegating the decision of what to do with her hair until she had put on her new navy suit. Cut fashionably several inches above the knee and hugging the slim curves of her hips, it fitted like a glove. She then decided to leave her golden mane loose, brushing it until it sang with electricity. Applying a hint of mascara to her thick lashes and just a touch of lipstick, she rushed out of the house wondering if all the trouble was going to be worth it. That voice on the phone had sounded so dull . . .

'Not bad . . . not bad at all!' Todd drawled appreciatively as she climbed into the open-topped sports car and snuggled down beside him. 'Just what sort of a job is this you're going for? Not this modelling stuff, is it?'

'Modelling? In the depths of the New Forest?' Tessa giggled, throwing back her head, feeling the wind whip her hair into ribbons as they gathered speed.

'Oh, don't look so stuffy, Todd! I told you ages ago I was thinking of a change.'

'But not all this way from Oxford, surely? You'll spend a fortune in fares.'

She decided not to mention the 'live-in' part. Instead she settled deeper in the seat. 'I haven't even got the job yet, so stop being so negative!'

En route her mind skimmed the phrasing of the advertisement in the *Veterinary Record*.

Opportunity to work with animals. Physical stamina, some veterinary experience necessary and flexibility essential. Live-in. Good wages to the right person.

Stamina she had oodles of. Hadn't she been taming two devils with reasonable success for the past decade? As for veterinary experience, she'd been three years with the Robert Marlowe Veterinary Hospital in Oxford — she could easily provide good references.

And the third requirement — flexibility? She was still mulling the word over when Todd finally spun the car on to a grass verge opposite a cluster of sleepy thatched cottages.

'Here we are. Beechwood Bridge — and half an hour early.' He sighed, leaning back in his seat, looking around disapprovingly. 'You can't honestly tell me you want a job here?'

'I think it's beautiful!' Tessa defended quickly, searching the dense foliage with eager eyes. 'Beechwood Hall is supposed to be at the end of the first track past the row of cottages . . . '

'There are small tracks everywhere!' Todd grumbled as they left the car on the verge and he took her arm. The village was small, but surprisingly busy. Workmen with ladders and bags of concrete and a large lorry with scaffolding all seemed to be converging in the one direction.

'Over there!' Tessa exclaimed excitedly, with a little jerk of her heart.

'I don't want you walking up a deserted

lane by yourself.' Todd frowned at the workmen. 'I'd better come.'

Tessa carefully dislodged the proprietorial hand from her waist. 'No, thank you, Todd. I'm quite capable!'

'I don't like the idea . . . ' He thrust his hands rebelliously in his pockets. 'OK. I'll go and find a petrol station, top her up, cruise around for a bit. Meet you here in an hour?'

Tessa watched him drive off. She didn't trust him not to hang around. Satisfied he had gone, she picked her way carefully over the uneven road surface where JCBs and diggers and immense terracotta pipes were lined along the pavements.

'Careful!' a voice boomed out at her feet.

Tessa almost jumped out of her skin as a face appeared from a hole just in front of her. She swayed on her high heels, nearly overbalancing.

'Didn't you see the sign? Why don't women ever look where they're going?'

Tessa mumbled an apology — and

immediately regretted it when she heard, 'Sorry's not going to do much good. I've lost the end of the rod, thanks to you.'

Men always got so cross when a job wasn't going right! Her father, being a builder, regularly fought with the complex arrangement of drains at home. A gaggle of long red rods often littered the drive. Building his own house in the sixties, Joe Dance's home had been his pride and joy, but the plumbing hadn't!

'It's a good idea to attach a piece of string from the rod to your arm and then if the rod slips in the drain you don't lose it completely,' she called to the dark head now absorbed with something at the bottom of the hole. 'Nine out of ten times it works.'

The head rose slowly — dangerously. Two large hands settled themselves on the outer rim of the hole. 'It's a bit late suggesting string! The damn thing's disappeared!'

'In that case, you need extended

rods. Obviously the blockage is further on than you estimated, or it might even be in a connecting drain.'

The head visibly bristled. She knew of course it was extremely unwise to offer constructive advice to a man trying to do a job he couldn't do. But, living with three males like her three, prudence ended with practicality. Her motto was, if a girl couldn't fix something herself never ask a man — unless there was absolutely no other reasonable alternative!

The mouth twitched. It was a good, firm mouth, with strong white teeth. 'Would you care to come down here and demonstrate?' he mumbled, drumming his fingers on the earth. 'As a mere amateur I'm obviously wasting my time.'

Tessa's fair eyebrows jerked together under her fringe. 'I'm not exactly dressed for DIY!'

He scowled, 'In that case, I'll just get on in my own way . . . that is, if there's nothing else I can help you with?'

She hesitated. 'Well . . . you might be able to actually. I'm looking for someone by the name of . . . Wilde?'

'Wilde? Are you sure that's the name?' He hoisted himself on to the side of the hole with powerful arms and she realised with a start that he was wearing only shorts. Her eyes spanned the bare, deeply tanned chest scattered with dark, curling hair. Reminding herself that she ought to be used to seeing half-naked men by now, she nevertheless found her gaze lingering, and it was quite an effort to drag it away. She disentangled her thoughts just quickly enough to catch the wry smile.

'I'm — er — more or less sure it was Wilde . . . ' she mumbled doubtfully.

'In that case, look no further. You've found him.' He clambered out of the hole and, standing at least a foot above her, chuckled, 'I'm afraid I can't exactly shake hands.'

Tessa felt her lower jaw drop, but managed to gasp, 'You're Mr Wilde, the

13

person I spoke to on the telephone . . . the person I made the appointment with?'

'Oh, no, that wasn't me.' He wiped his hands on a piece of cloth and stuffed it back into his shorts pocket. 'That would be Greeley — my secretary of sorts. He told me someone would be coming for an interview this morning — but I had no idea it was a woman.'

Tessa revived enough to wonder if this was sarcasm, but since the smile still touched his lips she decided to let it go. 'I'm Tessa Dance. And I'm half an hour early, I'm afraid.'

'Which is why,' he murmured, a frown pleating the dark brows together, 'you found me down there. We've had a problem with the water pressure and the guy who's doing the plumbing had a small accident on site yesterday.'

'Oh . . . ' Tessa smiled nervously. It wasn't the best way to begin an interview. Why hadn't she just kept quiet and walked past the hole?

'Did Greeley give you any details

about the advertised post?' he asked, his brown body glimmering under the sun.

She shook her head. 'No, but then I didn't ask for any. The line was terrible, I could barely hear him and I don't think he could hear me either.'

'The telephone wires need attention too,' he muttered, running a brown hand through untidy hair. 'You'd better come up to the house and I'll get changed.'

The drive was a long, winding one, with overgrown rhododendron bushes spilling on to the gravel and tall firs clustered behind them.

'You will have to ignore the state of the place,' he told her as they walked. 'I'm in the process of renovating Beechwood Hall and it's a mammoth task. At the same time, I'm trying to get my father's practice in the village on its feet. That's why I put an advertisement in the *Veterinary Record*.' He glanced ahead of him, nodding. 'There it is. Bit of a shock to the system, isn't it?'

She blinked just to make sure the

house was real. Sure enough, there were turrets and battlements and ivy-clad walls and far too many windows to count all at once. The great house looked very neglected but there was something about it . . .

She followed close on the heels of her guide ascending a flight of stone steps. They arrived at a heavy-looking wooden door and it creaked and juddered as he pushed it open.

'The family seat for four generations . . . Welcome to Beechwood Hall.'

Her heels rang on the stone flags as she walked in. Just as she imagined it from the outside . . . beams, dark-panelled walls and unsmiling portraits following the path of a never-ending staircase. Without warning two huge dogs charged across the flags.

'Juno! Jay! Sit!' her companion shouted.

They did as they were told and Tessa felt her legs come back to life with relief. 'Irish wolfhounds, aren't they? Are they friendly?'

'Once you've been introduced and made friends . . . yes.' He smiled.

She moved towards them and was soon lavished by licks and snuffles. 'They're gorgeous . . . so big!'

'You obviously get on with animals,' he said, watching her.

'I adore them.' Tessa stroked the bitch's head and the dog yawned, showing rather ancient molars. 'I've never had dogs of my own but I've been working with animals since I left school. These are a gorgeous pair . . . do they belong to Beechwood?'

'They were my father's dogs.' He flicked his eyes around the place. 'This is where I grew up — my father's house. He always intended to renovate Beechwood . . . but he died three months ago having hardly touched it.'

She looked up to say she was sorry, but saw him sprinting up the staircase. He called over his shoulder, 'If you would like to go ahead into that room on your left, I'll be with you shortly.'

As she ruffled the dog's coats, the

name of Wilde sent a sudden flash of recognition through her brain. She had seen a similar name in the newspapers recently . . .

Shrugging, she walked towards a set of doors. They looked heavy, but she gave a push and they swung open to reveal an astonishing room. Antique furnishings spilled from the walls and a very long polished table gleamed its way down the centre. Even the high ceiling had a fresco: tiny cherubs playing harps of gold.

'If you would like to take a seat?' a familiar voice said. The man she supposed was Greeley stood beside her, a tray of tea balanced on one hand. He was dressed in black, very formally, and with his expressionless face he looked the perfect example of a typical English butler, very reflective of the voice she'd heard on the phone.

Greeley set the tray on the table, and poured tea from the silver pot.

'Thank you,' Tessa said, looking at him under her lashes. He gave a curt little bow and disappeared. Not the best conversationalist in the world! she thought wryly, her eye sliding to a painting hanging over the fireplace. It's handsome subject, a man of mature years dressed in safari hat and shorts, held a baby chimpanzee in his arms.

'My father . . . Sir Gerald Wilde,' a voice said behind her.

She swung around to see her host dressed in a dazzling white shirt and casual slacks. 'Sir Gerald . . . then you're Samuel Wilde?'

He laughed, throwing back his head. 'I'm amazed a spot of dirt changes a man's appearance so radically.'

It wasn't just a spot, she thought, remembering the whorls of tight black hair covering a deeply tanned chest dusted with earth.

'If I had put my full name in the paper I would have been swamped with applications,' he explained, 'and for all the wrong reasons. Television has that effect on people.'

Her heart was beginning to palpitate.

Samuel Wilde — could it really be him? She had watched every one of his wildlife series, drooling at the mouth. 'I — er — seem to have made rather a bad start,' she mumbled.

'Please . . . don't let a little thing like telling a man his job disturb you.'

It wasn't what she had said which disturbed her, it was what she was thinking. Gorgeous and sexy were two adjectives which sprung readily to mind. Much more attractive than his television image, which wasn't surprising since, battling his way through bush and swamps, he hadn't been wearing clothes that clung to him like this. He was inches above Felix and Archie, and they were big enough. As for his age . . . it was difficult to determine. On television he looked about thirtyish, but now she could see he was older. There were interesting grooves in his cheeks and tiny laughter lines splayed under the tan at the corners of those hypnotic grey eyes.

'Do you think we might start afresh?'

he suggested efficiently. 'I'm Sam Wilde and you're Miss Dance. You work with animals . . . a VN, I take it?'

She nodded, still reeling from the shock.

He gave her an amused grin and pulled a chair from under the table, sitting down with a casual grace, like a cat lazily perching on a wall.

'Shall I begin, or would you prefer to go first?' he prompted.

'Oh, no, please, after you.'

He nodded. 'Very well. I'd like to know something about you. For a start, what prompted you to answer my advertisement?'

'Well, to be perfectly honest . . . ' she began enthusiastically, and then her voice trailed off. His eyes were roaming over the full thrust of her breasts exposed gently in the V of her suit. Sitting up straight, she ignored his amused expression. 'I — er — answered most of them actually, four in all.'

'All in the *Veterinary Record* or some under DIY?'

She felt her face burn. 'It seems

I'm not going to live that mistake down . . . '

'Oh, I've got a feeling you will,' he said drily. 'Do please continue. What was the fate of the other three?'

She eyed him warily. Was he being sarcastic? 'Two had already been filled,' she explained cautiously; 'the other involved reception and just a little nursing. I don't want part-time nursing, you see. I'm fully qualified.'

'So . . . you ended up with one interview?'

'And I almost didn't come, I have to admit. Your secretary didn't seem over-keen . . . '

He laughed, relaxing back in the chair. 'Oh, that was his best telephone voice, I can assure you.' Sam Wilde had a charming way with him, especially when he smiled like that. 'You say you're fully qualified?'

She opened her bag and drew out the reference Robert Marlowe had been kind enough to write for her.

'Hmm.' Sam Wilde arched a dark

eyebrow as he read. 'You've got your diploma in advanced veterinary nursing . . . frankly I can't see why you want to leave. Three years' experience with the hospital . . . the job seems pretty good to me.'

Tessa knitted her hands together in her lap. It was a good job; she'd worked hard for her diploma. Why should she be feeling so restless? Bob Marlowe had tried hard enough to talk her out of looking for another job . . . so had her family. Perhaps that was why she had made a firm decision. She had always put them first, made her life revolve around theirs. Now she was being selfish — and thoroughly enjoying it! She caught Samuel Wilde's stare and decided she wouldn't even try to explain, he wouldn't understand. 'I don't want to bore you with the details, Mr Wilde,' she said simply. 'In short, I suppose the answer is I really do want a change. I've lived in Oxford all my life. There's nothing wrong in looking further afield.'

'But to leave the city . . . come to a place like this? You're young. You won't find much of a social life in the middle of the Forest,' he pointed out.

Tessa shot a green-eyed glance across the polished table. 'It's not a social life I'm looking for. It's challenging work — with animals. I've never wanted to do anything else, not even when I was small.'

He smiled, one eyebrow quirking up. 'A woman who knows her mind.'

Tessa sat quietly, resisting the urge to agree with him.

'I need someone who will work hard,' he drawled slowly, emphasising the last word. 'The practice is a small one in the village, but demanding. My father let it run down badly. Having said that, it is coming along well.' He hesitated, looking at her with curious eyes. 'Another point . . . Beechwood Hall isn't very comfortable at the moment — I'm in the middle of renovations.'

'You mean . . . one would be required to live here, in Beechwood

Hall?' she asked, taken aback.

He nodded, obviously amused at her reaction. 'One would,' he repeated, mimicking her. 'Not a particularly attractive proposition, is it?'

'Well ... it isn't exactly what I expected ... '

'But the salary would compensate, of course.'

He was a strange man, on one hand making the job sound unattractive, almost as if he wanted to deter her, on the other inspiring an odd sense of intrigue. 'Would it be convenient to see the practice?' she asked.

'Sure.' He stood up. 'We'll take my car.'

Not a little headily Tessa followed him out of the house, her cool skin coming to life under the sun. The next moment she was sliding into the front seat of a deep red Porsche and being whisked along the drive to the village. When she came to climb out she wished she'd had more practice with Todd's low sports car, flushing under

Sam Wilde's amused scrutiny as she clung on to his offered hand. His grasp was firm, the fingers vibrantly strong. She was beginning to enjoy herself now.

'I'm re-equipping the practice,' he told her as they mounted a white painted veranda, 'so that if I decide to sell the business I can sell it as a going concern.'

'What a pity to sell such a lovely place,' Tessa gasped, glancing around at the heavy bowers of clematis cluttering the porch, almost obscuring the windows.

He gave a dismissive shrug. 'I'm considering the alternatives . . . I really haven't decided yet . . . which is another reason for my describing the job as I did — flexibility essential.'

'You mean, someone else might take the practice over?'

Those eyes caught her in their languid stare and her skin began to prickle. 'I've a busy practice in London to maintain apart from the TV work. So far I've been able to combine the two.

When my father died I had to turn my attention to Beechwood Bridge. I really don't know how long I'm going to be here.'

'You've someone running your London practice meanwhile?' she asked as they entered by a quaint half-glassed door that looked more like a grocery shop than a veterinary surgery.

'Paul Lancing, a friend of mine, is helping me out. I rely on him to locum for me when I'm away. Well, here we are. Beechwood Bridge Animal Clinic.'

It was an unpretentious, cosy room, with old benches and chairs that reminded her of school. The fresh white decorating and newly tiled floors shone out a welcome. 'What a surprise!' she exclaimed softly. 'It's so unusual. A curious mixture of old and new.'

'I wanted to retain its character. These cottages are three centuries old. Gus Allen isn't here today. If he were, he'd probably give you a detailed low-down on the history. Gus leased the practice from my father and lives with his wife Annie in the cottage next door. There is an adjoining wall, so we knocked a door into it for convenience's sake.'

'Is Gus going to stay on if you sell?'

'I suppose you could say both Gus and I are taking stock of the future. He's sixty and he could retire if he wanted. Though I'm not sure if Gus will ever do that; he's the kind who goes on forever.'

He stood with her, hands in pockets, his face relaxed. She could see the Samuel Wilde of the TV series, hawkish, charismatic, with those amazing grey eyes and unruly mass of chocolate-brown curls. She had never imagined she would actually be meeting him in real life . . .

'What do your family think of you leaving your job?' he asked out of the blue, giving her a little start.

'I haven't got around to mentioning it yet,' she admitted truthfully. 'I live with my father and twin brothers — they've a busy building yard between them. I don't suppose I shall be missed too much when I leave home.'

'I can't imagine that,' he answered in a wry tone as he pushed open the door to the theatre.

Her eyes grew wide as she followed him in. 'This is incredible . . . all new equipment?'

'I made the theatre my priority. Just air-conditioning to come.'

'You've worked very hard.'

'Flat-out.'

He showed her to the room he had converted into a makeshift office, though it was more like Aladdin's Cave, with boxes stacked to the ceiling, a desk toppling with papers and a word processor nosing up from a table-top. 'Do you know how to use one of those things?' he asked.

'Of course.' She looked askance at the chaos.

'I can put my finger on anything I want in this room, I can assure you,' he told her abruptly, picking up her thoughts.

She smiled, unperturbed. A few hours in here and she would soon have it sorted out! 'And staff . . . have you anyone else to help?'

'Gus's wife — Annie. She's not a qualified VN, not that you would notice. Animals are second nature to her after so many years. As far as Beechwood Hall goes, I've no staff who live in, with the exception of Greeley. My father's cook and a few women come in from the village on a daily basis to clean.'

A soft padding came from the veranda and they swivelled around. 'Juno! What the devil are you doing here?' The dog tried to slink in, her nose in the crack of the door and Sam walked to open it fully, brushing his hand affectionately over her wiry coat. 'She's an escape artist. Even Greeley can't stop her when she's determined.'

Tessa noticed again the inferior condition of her teeth as she yawned. 'Oh, dear, poor Juno,' she let out before she could stop herself.

Sam Wilde frowned. 'Her teeth, you mean? Yes, they are a pretty horrible mess, aren't they? I'm going to start treatment with her soon. What would you diagnose as the problem, Miss Dance?'

Tessa bent down and gently eased Juno's mouth open to get a better look. 'There's a good girl,' she soothed, squinting in, 'just open a little wider.' She could see the dog was nervous, as any human would be with decaying dentine. 'Caries, isn't it?' Tessa ventured.

'Hmm. Very good. What made you spot it?'

Tessa staightened her back and looked for a washbasin. 'I took a course during my training. Canine dentistry always attracted me and Robert Marlowe gave me plenty of practice once he knew I was interested in the work.'

He led her into the next room and watched her as she rinsed her hands. 'You actually enjoyed canine dentistry?' he asked with surprise.

'Very much.'

'Unusual for a woman.'

'No,' she differed firmly. 'Not these days.' She disposed of her wet hands with a paper towel and glanced up at the dark, brooding features, her mind and body suddenly in upheaval at having his presence so near.

'I still can't understand why you are interested in a temporary job offering no security and no social distractions. I don't think it would suit you, to be quite honest,' he told her sharply.

Taken aback Tessa felt naked hostility surface behind those grey eyes — or was it a mixture of suspicion and dislike? But what had she done to incur it?

'To be equally honest, Mr Wilde, I don't think you can judge a person's suitability in a half-hour interview. That's hardly fair.'

'And what would you suggest, in that case?' he retorted with a slight sneer.

'A couple of weeks' trial period,' she suggested bravely, wondering if she had heard herself say that.

He shook his head. 'That wouldn't be much help to you. The upheaval of making the break from home and having to go back if things didn't work out would hardly be worth the bother, would it?'

It was perceptive of him, she had to give him that, to see into her circumstances. But she had the feeling he wasn't thinking of her in the least. Those eyes told a different tale.

He stiffened, a mask settling over his face. 'Is there anything else you would like to ask me?'

Was this a dismissal?

'N-no,' she stammered foolishly, wishing she could prevent Sam Wilde from putting an end to what had seemed a promising opportunity.

'No doubt your family would object profoundly to your taking on such a position as this. There is the problem of the media, for instance. Reporters might involve you in some bad Press if they discovered you staying in Beechwood Hall . . . alone . . . with me.'

Obviously she had failed the interview with flying colours! But did he really have to palm her off with such feeble excuses?

'I'll show you out,' he offered coolly.

She shook her head. 'I know the way, thank you. Goodbye, Mr Wilde.'

She hurried to escape, her cheeks flaring pink, promising herself that never again would glamour deceive her — on or off the screen. As far as celebrities went, if Sam Wilde was a fair example, the world of entertainment was welcome to keep them!

2

Tessa watched, fascinated.

Sam Wilde's fingers were long and brown and had the deep, narrow lines carved into them that spoke of hard, outdoor living. Yet, working with extreme gentleness on the collie's thin body laying on the operating table, he could have been painting the most delicate of pictures.

Was it a week since she had moved into Beechwood Hall?

How had it all come about after that first disastrous interview? Her mind wandered from the operating table and alighted on the evening three weeks ago when she had returned from Beechwood Bridge.

'It was too far away, Tess,' her brother Felix had muttered in a clumsy attempt to comfort her. 'You'll easily find another job locally.'

'And who would . . . ?' Archie began, surveying the lounge piled high with magazines, discarded sweaters and squash rackets.

'Look after you if I weren't here?' Tessa supplied with a rueful grin.

'That's not the point. We don't know a thing about him!' Joe Dance protested. 'He might look all right on the television, but in real life . . . ?'

Tessa had listened silently as the rest of the household pronounced judgement and then happily dispersed to carry on with their lives.

Perhaps it was all for the best, she'd consoled herself. But over the next few days she had begun wishing she had made more of an effort at the interview. It was his attitude she took exception to. If she had spoken up for herself, not let him manipulate the conversation, she was sure she could have got the job.

When the telephone had rung the following weekend she had listened in shock to Samuel Wilde's voice. Was she still interested? How soon could she start?

'Scalpel please, Tessa.'

She passed the instrument, feeling a minute brush of his fingers against hers. Their eyes locked briefly.

'How is our patient?' He glanced over the collie's inert body.

'He's doing fine . . . ' They drifted quietly on through the operation, Tessa responding automatically to his commands. Occasionally she smiled to herself, thinking that this was Sam Wilde, the television celebrity. Naturally enough she'd been nervous at first, but the ease with which she had settled in had frightened her. Was she really so relieved to leave home and adopt a new way of life? Or was Sam Wilde the challenge she had been looking for?

'It's like an oven in this place!' he groaned, and she glanced at her employer and saw a fine row of perspiration glistening on the strong, tanned forehead. Taking a small pad from the trolley, she leant across without obstructing him and dabbed. For a moment, she was stunned by the contact of his body, even through gloves and the pad. His eyes came up to meet hers, deep grey pools that always caught her off guard.

'Thanks.'

She smiled. It was the first physical contact between them. But she had made the same action dozens of times in her working life . . . what in heaven's name was she dwelling on it for? Perhaps it was the heat. They were almost in June now and temperatures in the little cottage practice, which faced south, were high.

He seemed to be thinking along the same lines too, for he murmured, 'We'll have the air-conditioning in soon. Lord knows how Gus has managed all these years without it.'

Tessa thought of the older man who had run the surgery for the last two decades. It was typical of him not to worry over a minor problem like air-conditioning. A reliable source of tea and home-made cake was of greater concern.

Tessa smoothed the area around the wound as Sam began the suturing. 'I've enjoyed working with Gus this week,' she said enthusiastically. 'He and Annie are really lovely people.'

He turned his head, his grey eyes calm. 'Good. I'm glad to hear you're getting on so well.'

She refrained from further small talk, allowing him to complete the suturing in full concentration. He made small, neat sutures, taking infinitesimal care. When he finished tying the last one, he glanced up at her. 'That's it, more or less.'

She studied the row of stitches. 'You make it seem like a work of art, not a surgical operation.'

He grinned, shrugging her compliment off. 'Oh, it's straightforward enough with the right equipment. I'm beginning to see how handicapped Gus has been. Major ops he's had to refer to the vet fifteen miles away. Not forgetting, of course, that I've found myself some competent help at last.'

Tessa hoped he couldn't see her sudden flush. It was rewarding to have a compliment returned, but it was also unnerving — the interview had been such a catastrophe! And it wasn't only first impressions. She had associated him with exotic animals and glamorous women, not with mundane jobs like Parvo injections and boosters! TV had a strange way of making people seem like gods, unapproachable and remote. Perhaps that was why every so often she felt like pinching herself just to see if she was dreaming.

Thank goodness she had persuaded the twins and Todd not to drive her down. Egos would have clashed madly! They were about as much in favour for her working for him as they were for her entering a convent — and no doubt would have loved the chance to tell him so!

'I don't like it,' Joe Dance had persisted. 'Casanovas, these characters. I've seen their type before!'

Her eyes drifted downwards to the dog and the steady, reassuring fingers taking such care. Casanova or not, he was the most accomplished professional she had ever worked with.

'We'll take him to a recovery cage,' Sam pondered beside her. 'I want to make sure he comes around OK, but I've a problem. Unfortunately I have to be at the house for six to see the builders before they leave . . . '

'I'll be here,' she offered immediately. 'Are you concerned he may need an injection of heart stimulant?'

'Mmm. I've given him one, but another might be necessary.'

Tessa knew she was quite capable of doing this, but it was customary for the vet to watch over his patient until he was satisfied the animal was in safe recovery.

'How about if we compromise?' she suggested. 'I'll check him every few minutes. If I see any sign of deterioration I'll knock for Gus. After all, he only lives through the adjoining door.'

Relief spread over his face and he smiled at her. 'Done! Do you just want to go and check he's there? I'll get our patient into a recovery cage meanwhile.'

She watched him gently pick up the collie, marvelling at the tenderness of those large arms and the graceful sway of the tall, muscular body which moved in a loose-limbed stride across the floor.

'Want some help with the drip?' she called, as he suddenly hesitated in a complex arrangement of tubes.

'You're not supposed to read my thoughts . . . yet!' he answered with a grin.

'It's impossible not to. That's what I'm trained for.'

'I guess I'm just not used to a double act,' he answered rather roughly, surprising her. He turned away and she felt a sudden tension in the air between them. She had only been joking. There was no question of her crowding him.

When she arrived back from confirming the arrangement with Gus, the collie was sleeping peacefully in a recovery cage and Sam was bending over him. When he glanced up, she was relieved to see a smiling row of white teeth — television teeth, she had privately named them!

'Greeley has arranged the meal with Mrs Pearson for eight-thirty,' he told her. 'Does that give you enough time to get back to Beechwood and change?'

'Yes, plenty.'

He made to leave, hanging his white coat on the old-fashioned hall stand which no one had had the heart to throw out during the redecorating of the surgery. 'Tessa, thanks for all your hard work this week.'

She smiled, her green eyes sparkling. 'I've loved every minute of it.' And it was true, she had. In spite of the bad start, it had developed into an exhilarating first week.

'And — er — one thing more,' he added hesitantly. 'I've company coming tomorrow. Gus is going to cover my Saturday morning in surgery. I'd like you to be here to help him if that's possible.'

'Yes — yes, of course . . . '

When he had gone she let out a long breath. Sometimes she felt she was treading on glass. He was a strange man. And suddenly to tell her about 'company' like that . . . it was mildly irritating, too, to be given such a large hint that he would be otherwise occupied and wouldn't want to be disturbed!

Tessa sighed, turning back to her patient, telling herself not to be so insanely sensitive and not to get too involved. Hadn't things gone well up to now?

She began clearing away with an added spurt of enthusiasm, casting her mind back over the familiar pattern of days: breakfast with Mrs Pearson in the kitchen, soaking up a deluge of village gossip, mornings assisting Gus, afternoons with Sam. He made it plain, too, that he expected her company at dinner. Every evening they sat at the ridiculously long banqueting table, waited on by Greeley who moved around the room like a magician, producing silver tureens from out of nowhere.

'S-a-m . . . ' She coiled her tongue around the three letters. Much better than Samuel. And much less formal than Mr Wilde, which they had dispensed with in the first hour of working together.

At seven, Gus Allen poked his head around the door. Short and stocky, he made up for his lack of height with a deep bass voice. 'How's the patient doing?' he enquired, frowning at the collie.

'Into a perfectly normal sleep now, Gus. I don't think he'll need another injection.'

'That's good. Want any help?' He came in and stood beside her, running a plump hand through the remainder of his grey hair.

'Well, I rather think Sam would like it if I said you'd checked him thoroughly before I left.'

'Gone up to the Hall, has he?'

She nodded. 'He's still fighting with the builders, I think. The carpenters want to use a certain type of wood and Sam's against it. He says it's ecologically unsuitable. I heard them arguing about it this morning.'

Gus smiled vaguely. 'Trees! Gerry's obsession too. It's just a heck of a shame he never managed to settle in Beechwood Bridge. Always told me that when his appetite for travelling diminished he was going to settle down, renovate the Hall and run the practice properly.'

'Didn't it ever happen?'

Gus shook his head, frowning. 'Gerry ended up virtually penniless. Got stung by his ex-wife for a fortune in maintenance.'

'You mean Sam's mother?' Tessa asked incredulously.

'Oh, no, not Else. Else divorced Gerry when Sam was five. She was Swedish — decided to go back to her own country. By that time she had met someone else. Gerry's trips abroad left her desperately lonely. But as far as Sam was concerned, Gerry wouldn't let her take him out of Britain.'

'So he married for the second time?' Tessa persisted, her curiosity overwhelming her.

Gus looked up. 'Unfortunately . . . yes. Kay was thirty years his junior and quite a corker. His intention was to settle down at Beechwood, but it never happened. Predictably their marriage didn't last long . . . they divorced and it cost him everything.'

Tessa's eyes grew wider by the minute. 'What a story!'

'Indeed . . . indeed. My old friend, you see, seemed to be attracted by the wrong sort of woman.'

Gus held his hands up in horror. 'Just look at all these lights and dials,' he sighed. 'More radar screens than in an aeroplane cockpit!'

Tessa grinned. 'You'll get used to it all.'

'I'm not so sure. It makes you feel a

darned sight older when you're confronted with a room full of machines
you can't even turn on.' He slid a grin
in her direction. 'But then, why should
I bother when I've got a beautiful
young head like yours to think for me?
Come on, now, let's see to this laddie
here, whom our Sam has worked
wonders upon.'

And, with another deep sigh, he
pulled a stethoscope out of his pocket
and applied it to the warm, regularly
lifting chest.

★ ★ ★

'You haven't eaten your meal.' Sam
glanced at her plate. 'Not sickening for
something?'

Tessa shook back her hair. She stared
back at him. 'It's the heat, I suppose. In
here it's cool . . . but you know how the
temperature soars in the surgery.'

'That's a pitiful excuse!' He scowled
at her, resting his elbows on the table.
'You're far too thin as it is. What will

your father say if you go home as skinny as a rake? Your family's opinion of me is running at an all-time low to begin with.'

'How do you know that?'

'It's what you haven't said that worries me. You talk about everything under the sun, except the people who are closest to you. I'm right, aren't I? They don't like you working for the infamous Samuel Wilde?'

She grinned, her eyes widening. 'And are you infamous?'

There was hardly any hesitation in his answer. 'I might be thought of as such — in some circles.'

'Goodness . . . such honesty!'

'Don't be too smart, Tessa; I might be a dangerous man.'

She shook her head slowly, almost laughing. 'I don't think so. I trust you.'

He looked at her for a long time. 'You shouldn't trust me. In fact, you shouldn't trust any man you've only known a week.'

'I've known you three in all. And

you're a vet. You've an ethical code to keep,' she teased.

'Very touching.' He leaned back in his chair, eyeing her speculatively. 'Would you be surprised if I told you that my one and only candidate for the job was you?'

The wind was taken out of her sails. 'You mean . . . no one else was interested — only me?'

'No one. And, what was worse, you were a woman.' He tilted his head, still watching her. 'Now you can accuse me of sexual discrimination. Because I have to admit, when I placed that advertisement, I was thinking along the lines of a male student filling in time.'

'If you're trying to shock me, it won't work.' Her eyes twinkled disbelievingly. 'I think you're trying to provoke a reaction from me . . . because you aren't used to being accepted at face value.'

'Oh? And what is my face value?'

She sighed lightly, the laughter ebbing at the back of her throat.

'Exactly what I've experienced this week. You're a man who loves animals.'

He gazed at her, shaking his head. 'Tessa, don't be so naïve! Don't you know everyone has a different side to them? Don't you think you're being just a little too sure of yourself thinking of me as some kind of glorified Noah?'

Unwilling to take him seriously, she shrugged, hoping he couldn't see how nervous he was beginning to make her feel. 'You made it quite clear at the interview what the pitfalls were, Sam. Patently clear. I'm not expecting anything from this job other than day-to-day experience. All my life I've been organised, structured, kept within the framework of family and work, concerned with Archie and Felix and my father. I'm enjoying myself now . . . even though I know it won't last, that in a few months I'll probably be looking for another job. But I'm not worried — why should you be?'

He groaned, lifting his grey eyes up. 'For exactly the reasons you've expressed!

My God, why did I do it? Why did I phone you?'

'Because you had no one else, so you said. I don't blame you for employing me as a last resort. In fact, now I view it as a sort of challenge. I want to show you I'm good at the job — and I know I am.'

He looked at her, shaking his head again. 'This conversation is getting us nowhere. You just don't understand, Tessa. Or you choose to ignore what I'm trying to say to you.' Digging his hands deeply into his pockets, he got up from the table and walked slowly to stare out of one of the windows. She knew she was frustrating him. But why? She was under the assumption that he had been pleased with her this week. It just seemed to faze him more when she told him how much she enjoyed the job.

The Great Hall suddenly seemed vast and lonely. Only Sir Gerald radiated a supportive smile. It was funny how things became more evident as you got to know someone, Tessa thought as she watched Sam. Tall, erect, earth-brown curls dominating the overall effect, sweeping down into a crop at the base of his neck . . . no one could mistake him for anyone but his father's son. But maybe that was all part of the frustration — trying to live up to expectations, living here, building up a practice he really had no interest in . . . to his father's memory.

What did Sam really want out of life for himself? To travel, to be free, to give his time to the London practice, or simply just to be a celebrity . . . would he settle for that alone?

'I did wonder why you offered me the job,' she said, sighing, hoping to rectify the uneasy atmosphere before the end of the evening. 'You've been very honest. You needn't have told me.'

He rounded on her, the angles of his face harsher, even menacing. 'Your simplicity amazes me! I've been no-where near honest! Men rarely are.'

She looked at him, a little hurt but she wasn't going to show it. 'You're telling me you don't want me to trust you, is that it?'

'You could put it like that.'

'Do you expect me to pack my bags and run?'

'You're being flippant. I'm just warning you . . . don't bank on me to act like a saint. I'm averse to being committed — in any sense of the word.'

'And what makes you think I want a commitment?' she asked, beginning to flounder.

'Because I've learned that women like you usually do.'

Tessa gasped, her green eyes amazed. 'Women like me! And what do you mean by that?'

'Organised women. You told me yourself you come from a framework — you're family-orientated. You like life cut and dried, safe and secure — including your men.'

'That's ridiculous!' she burst out, scarlet fanning her cheeks.

'Aren't you just the least bit worried about staying here alone with me?' he persisted, disappearing out of her vision. Unless she twisted around in her seat she couldn't see him. He was deliberately trying to scare her!

She sat quite still, listening, her hands folded in her lap, unwilling to crane her neck around. She could feel the electricity permeating her back. 'You're not frightening me, Sam.'

'Frighten you?' he laughed cynically. 'I don't want to frighten you. I want you to be realistic, to come down from that ivory tower of yours.'

A drumbeat sprang into her veins and she felt the skin of her neck twist. 'I'm not worried about living in the same house as you and you can't make me say I am,' she said defiantly.

'I'm a very gregarious man,' he whispered, his mouth close by her ear.

'You're a vet,' she reminded him firmly, 'with a vocation.'

'I'm not just a vet,' he contradicted her hotly. 'I work very hard in television trying to get over a serious subject to the public. It's a totally different world

. . . the environment tends to change people.'

'I . . . I suppose so . . . I don't understand how TV works. But I do know that if you are destined to cure and save life you can't suffocate your gift. It's like having plastic surgery. The outer appearance changes, but inwardly you're still the same person.'

She was not ready for what happened next. He swung her around by her shoulders making her jump, his hands hot on her skin.

'You're determined to stick to your guns, aren't you?' His breath and the unevenness of his voice made her body melt where she sat, feeling her nerve-ends throb at the contact of his fingers. 'You've got me neatly pigeonholed into the category of person you'd like to see me as.'

'No! That's not true!' she exclaimed, briefly tempted to argue with him. But, when his hand began to stroke her arms and run through her hair, something crazy happened inside her, something she had never experienced before. She couldn't move. Her heart was jerking from one side of her body to the other and little white dots seemed to be plaguing her vision as she forced open her eyes, staring at him.

'You're very beautiful, very fresh. I haven't met anyone quite like you . . . ' His hands were caressing her arms, gently, slowly rubbing at the fabric of her skin. 'You're a challenge to me, Tessa.'

She managed, somehow, to keep outwardly calm. She must deny she was attracted to him, common sense told her that; this was all part of a game. It meant nothing — just a challenge; he had bluntly told her so. But before she could speak he lifted her to her feet, drawing her firmly to him as though she were a doll. 'Let me clarify the situation.'

It was like being caught in the glare of oncoming traffic. Unable to move, stunned by the light, she was transfixed as he cupped her chin with his hand.

'You're not going to stop me?' he asked, grinning.

She opened her mouth to say she was, but her mind had shut down, effectively cutting off speech. Instead, the mechanics of her brain decreed that her eyes close and her body shudder expectantly.

His lips were hungry, the full, sensual mouth covering hers with a violent pressure. Was this what she wanted? she heard a little voice asking. The answer swam discordantly in her brain, lost somewhere in no man's land between ecstasy and desperation.

Her mouth opened in an agony of desire against a kiss which was tantalising, enhancing the hardness of his chest against her breasts. It was as though she retained no strength to push him away. Not that she wanted to. Drowning like this, under his lips . . . hadn't she from the first wondered what it would be like to be kissed by Sam Wilde?

Her body arched as his lips sought the bare skin of her shoulders, teasing an erotic line to her throat. As he reached her softly parted mouth she heard his deep sigh, almost a groan.

Lost in a new, trembling excitement, it was seconds before she woke to the distant movement in the background. Sam was drawing away . . . his hands slipping from her body.

'What is it?' she heard him mutter impatiently.

As though drugged, she turned her head and her eyes collided with Greeley's. How long had he been there, watching them? Flushing heavily, she came to her senses, recoiling, holding on to one of the chairs for support as her mind spun.

'It's the telephone, sir,' Greeley intoned without expression. 'Miss Nina Graham, to enquire after the weekend's arrangements.'

Stunned, Tessa tried to think what had happened over the last few moments. Since her mind was no more than jelly she was relieved when Juno and Jay bounded in, enabling her to use the distraction to recover, catching Sam's last few words over her heartbeat.

' . . . so tell Nina I'll ring her back, will you, Greeley? Sometime later tonight.'

'Don't look so embarrassed, Tessa.' Sam drawled after the man had gone. 'Greeley is very discreet. Though I have to admit the Great Hall is hardly the place for this. Much better to adjourn upstairs.' He laughed, his grey eyes mocking. 'Or did I just misread what happened?'

It was true, she had wanted him to kiss her, but his idea of lovemaking was a physical quest, a challenge, nothing more. And that was not what she wanted even though her body might have responded momentarily.

She nodded, her lips dry. 'I . . . did want you to kiss me,' she admitted, her lids wet with perspiration as she tried to focus on him.

'And?'

This wasn't the man she had worked

with all week — or was it? This was a man who had probably successfully seduced every woman he had ever wanted because of who he was. And yet in the last seven days she had stupidly hoped he was different. But, to be fair, hadn't she been flirting with him a little tonight . . . just a little? And hadn't he tried to warn her? Surely that little demonstration was convincing enough. He had not lied to her. He had been painfully truthful, making his intentions perfectly plain. Now she must do the same. She must remember who Samuel Wilde was and what he expected of women.

'Sam . . . don't waste your time on me,' she pleaded shakily. 'I'm not excusing myself for letting you kiss me like that . . . and I just wish it hadn't happened, but it has . . . and now I think we had better try to forget it.'

'Forget it?' She could feel the vibes of his anger — and she was afraid, truly afraid.

'Forget it . . . yes, because . . . ' She

searched frantically for the words to convince him. 'Because you're right, I am a stranger in your world. And because I'm serious about my job. I want to hold on to it, for however long it might last.' Brave words, she thought, panic-stricken.

Shock registered on his face. 'My God, Tessa, you're a cool one!'

She wondered then if he was going to grab her. She could either scream or submit — and just the memory of that kiss lingering on her lips was enough to tell her which choice she would make . . . with his persuasion.

She edged towards the door. Would he let her out? Jay and Juno nudged her fingertips as she went. Somehow they gave her added confidence.

At the door, she realised she was safe. Perhaps she had even worried for nothing. She had better try to put things right before the morning if she valued the job she had just been talking about.

'Sam?'

He didn't reply, just turned his back and surveyed the dark night through the window but she could see his profile, hard as granite.

'Goodnight, Sam,' she said softly, walking out, blood drumming at her temples. When she had climbed the stairs and entered her bedroom, a flight up from his, she locked the door and, with her back to it, closed her eyes and allowed herself free rein to tremble from head to toe.

What on earth was she doing here?

What was she doing alone — almost — in the house of a man who, if he had wanted to tonight, could have forced his will over hers? And the one statement he had made which had really found its target was when he'd told her she had him neatly pigeon-holed into a category. She had wanted him to be something he was not. And he had perceived that error . . . and in his own way tried to make her see it too.

Letting out a painful breath, Tessa

searched for a tissue and blew her nose resolutely.

The voice of reason sounded, comfortingly, within her. Now the inevitable pass was over and dealt with, it said, she could get on with her job without any emotional vibes zinging around the place and destroying her confidence — or any misunderstandings between them.

Sam would simmer down.

In a couple of days, things would be back to normal . . .

3

Tessa discovered next morning that Sam had simmered down sooner than she expected.

Simmered enough to be strolling with a blonde on the lawns of Beechwood, laughing and joking.

She watched them, peering out from one of the Great Hall windows. Her sense of relief came in an unusual form. A sort of juggling about of inner parts in the pit of her stomach.

She rushed her breakfast with Mrs Pearson and left for the practice, telling herself she was pleased. The distraction had come just at the right time.

At eleven, as she was wrestling with a Labrador called Frankie on the threshold of the surgery, trying to coax him in, the dark red Porsche purred to a stop in the roadway.

'Sam and his lady-friend,' Gus

muttered, squeezing past her. 'You get Frankie into the surgery and I'll be back in a mo.'

By the time she persuaded the dog in, scooped her hair out of her eyes in order to get a look at the car from the window, Gus was waving goodbye.

'Phew!' He chased in. 'They're going to London, apparently. Nina has decided she doesn't fancy a survival weekend at the Hall.' Tessa clung on to Frankie, oddly disappointed.

'You've met Nina, haven't you?' Gus asked, fixing a keen eye on Frankie. Without waiting for an answer he bent down and gently eased the fur back from an abscess threatening to form by Frankie's tail. 'Hmm. Not too bad; I think we'll try some medication first, rather than anything more drastic. Nina's the assistant to the producer on Sam's wildlife series. Went to the Masai game reserve with him last year. Bright girl.'

Tessa listened, totally at sea with the way she felt. If she didn't know better

66

she would think she had the nasty stirrings of jealousy — but she did know better. Sam was hard as rock, very convincing and so smooth. Last night meant nothing, just a distraction to him since he had nothing else better to do than to provoke her.

Despite her rational thinking, the vision of Nina and Sam in the Porsche lodged, obstinately, in her mind all day. And all through the lonely meal at Beechwood that night and through Sunday when she slipped back to the surgery on the pretext of checking the collie.

Gus discovered her there and insisted she stay to tea, and Annie cheerfully made scones and topped them up with strawberry jam and ice-cream.

It was late when she started back to Beechwood. A cool breeze had sprung up and she shivered in her thin summer frock. She had grown used to the long drive now . . . would she see Sam's car at the top of it, parked next to Nina's white one? But all she discovered was the white coupé.

Greeley met her on the cold flags of Beechwood. 'Mrs Pearson has left you a salad selection tonight, Miss Tessa.' At least he had warmed enough to compromise and not call her Miss Dance any longer. 'Shall I serve right away?'

'Is Mr Wilde back yet?' she asked, already knowing the answer.

'I'm afraid not. Mr Wilde rang to say he will be staying overnight in London.'

'Oh.' Her heart sank. Why had she imagined Sam would come home tonight? What reason was there for him to come back? Certainly not her. 'Well, no, thank you, Greeley,' she managed, her voice thin. 'I've eaten already, with Mr and Mrs Allen; I couldn't manage any more.'

With a ghost of a smile — or grimace? — Greeley disappeared into the shadows. She decided to walk along to the smallest of Beechwood's recreation-rooms. Though it was summer, most of the house resembled a fridge.

But in here it was snug, filled with books and stout, lumpy cushions. Juno and Jay were already there, guarding the scarlet logs of a blazing fire. They trotted to meet her, thumping their tails furiously. After playing with the dogs for a while, she coiled herself into an old leather sofa with horsehair grinning from its seams. The flickering shadows of fire-light cast themselves across the room and the dogs, sensing she was settled, lay down too and began to snore.

Her mind strayed to the dozens of empty rooms above and beyond. Beechwood Hall must have been a wonderful place in its day, when Else and Gerry were first married. Mrs Pearson, who had been in service with the Wildes for years, had told her some of the stories of the elegant balls they'd held in the now disused ballroom. Despite Sam not returning and the emptiness of the rest of the house, she felt strangely, inexplicably, at home.

She thought of Sam's kiss. When she closed her eyes, his fingers were running over her skin again, his mouth covered her lips and his heart beat again, against hers.

It was here, on the sofa, that she fell asleep in front of the roaring fire dreaming of Sam ... and where Greeley gently awoke her, before she foggily climbed the stairs and, after slipping off her clothes, fell straight into bed.

$$\star \quad \star \quad \star$$

Sam's grey eyes were frosted with tiredness.

Tessa didn't feel at all sorry for him. People who burned the candle at both ends were bound to be tired, even exhausted. He should have come home from London earlier, instead of rushing back this morning. She wondered if Nina Graham had returned with him and if she was staying on at the Hall. But Sam made no mention of Nina as he strolled into the surgery.

Juno padded beside him, her panting

heavy in the midday heat. Sam sank into a seat and smiled. 'Well, Tessa, tell me everything! Every little detail of your weekend.'

So, this was how it was to be. As though nothing had happened. Well, that was what she wanted too, wasn't it? Business as usual?

She flicked through her notes, keeping her eyes down on the paper. 'We had a busy Saturday morning in surgery. A Labrador with an abscess . . . several Parvos . . . a spaniel whose paw had been caught in a trap. Luckily the dog survived and Gus thinks the wound will heal, but his owner, Mr Hawkins, is worried there may be more of the traps scattered around.'

Sam got up from his chair. 'Tom Hawkins? No doubt the traps were left for badgers or foxes in his part of the woods. Why in heaven's name do people do it? It's brutal torture . . . ' His face grew dark. 'I'll call in and have a chat with Tom later. Anything else?'

She glanced back to her notes. 'Late

71

on Saturday afternoon a pony was knocked — not badly, fortunately.'

'In the village?' he asked, concerned.

'Yes, by the ford . . . '

'Did Gus go out?'

Tessa nodded. She could see he was very disturbed. 'Thankfully the pony was only bruised; the car damaged the wooden bridge more than anything else. But I think Gus informed the Forestry Commission people all the same.'

He frowned deeply and she knew he was angry. Cars speeding through the Forest were one of the main causes of accidents with animals and very often pedestrians. Though he refrained from commenting, she knew what was going on in his mind.

'No problems on Sunday?'

'No . . . none at all. Annie said not even a phone call.'

He glanced at his watch. 'Have you much on this morning?'

'Just open surgery with Gus.'

'In that case, if he can cope, I would

like to crack on with Juno's problem. Greeley said she hasn't eaten . . . and our new dental equipment has arrived, so it seems an opportune time to have her in.'

'Don't you have . . . other commitments today?' she enquired diplomatically.

He laughed. 'You mean Nina? Oh, no. She came back with me this morning just to collect her car.'

Tessa nodded, feeling the beginnings of the old excitement of knowing they were going to work together and, very selfishly, that he would not have to hurry away to entertain a guest.

Sam's hand slipped down to fondle Juno's head and the dog looked up at him as if she understood what he was saying. 'She's nervous,' he murmured. 'It's incredible how they know, isn't it?'

Tessa knelt and ruffled her coat, avoiding Sam's large brown hand, his fingers sinking into the wiry brush at her haunches. 'Good girl,' Tessa whispered.

Out of the blue Sam asked, 'How did

you manage at Beechwood over the weekend?'

She got up, smoothing down her green uniform. 'Perfectly, thanks.'

'Hmm. Most women would have objected to being left alone there.'

'I wasn't alone. I had the dogs — and Greeley, of course.'

'A lot of women wouldn't have liked that much either,' he chuckled, grinning at her.

It was as though Friday night was completely forgotten. Had his weekend with Nina been successful enough to erase it from his mind? An answering smile curved her lips, and as he looked at her with those grey eyes she felt colour flying up her face to her hairline.

'Right . . . let's see what we can do. Perhaps you can ask Annie to take the telephone and any other calls?' he said, getting to his feet, stretching his long brown body in front of her, and she hid her continuing flush by hurrying through to Gus and giving him the orders of the day.

In Theatre, she relaxed, concentrating on preparation. She enjoyed canine dentistry and it would be interesting to observe Sam's method of working. It was not an easy operation by any means. She'd had enough experience to know that many vets avoided this sphere of surgery although, defying common belief, many techniques in human dentistry could, with a little modification, be used on pets.

A few moments later Sam appeared behind her, dressed in his surgical gown, moving about the room with quiet detachment, but an energy which radiated his need to get on with the job in hand.

'I'm sure I don't have to go through the routine with you,' he murmured as he checked the instruments. 'I'll probably be using glass ionomers to release fluoride. That'll help to strengthen the dentine and prevent further spread. And then composite or amalgam ... you're conversant with this procedure?'

'Yes,' she answered, her green eyes calm.

She gave a small inward sigh of relief as they began working on Juno. She listened attentively, passing him the respective tools, though very often he had no need to ask as she premeditated his moves. He took her through the stages with cool deliberation, clarifying specific points. Nothing was rushed. Nothing seemed impossible as she watched him, even Juno's diabolical tooth problem.

'A horrible mess,' Sam declared eventually as he displayed an exposed root.

She drew closer and felt the instant effect of his body, like fizzy lemonade running over her spine. Blinking, she tried hard to keep her eyes fixed on the dog's open mouth, remembering she was here in a professional capacity. It wasn't easy. Her lids felt heavy as she tried all the harder to concentrate.

'Caries is often identified when the dog yawns, as you first saw it,' he murmured, delicately investigating the tooth with poised fingers, his brow in a pleat.

She blinked hard again, listening to the tone of his voice. 'Here, on the biting surfaces of the molars.' Sam gestured to the spot. She edged in a little closer, viewing the dull white powdery-looking area which appeared to be staining yellow and brown, sensing the fine downy hairs on her arms meeting the thicker, coarser ones on his; she moved sharply away.

'The lesions would eventually turn black,' he told her, unaware, it seemed of her movement. 'Decay penetrates the pulp and a painful tooth abscess results. Now, would you like to prepare the drill for me? And we'll attempt to see just how much we can do.'

When Tessa watched Sam work she was hard put to it to remember the man who had goaded and frightened her. In an obscure way animals seemed to supersede humans for him. Had he been hurt so badly in the past that he couldn't forgive and forget? Tangled emotional attitudes, she knew through experience, only clarified if you talked about them, as she had been able to do after her mother died. The counselling she and the twins had received had proved invaluable. The worst thing to have happened to them as a family would have been to bottle up their grief and anger and, worst of all, guilt.

Had Sam bottled up his emotions from the time Else left him? Repressed them so deeply in childhood that he couldn't relate with women properly in maturity? Perhaps glamour and sophistication was a safe level on which to function. And that would explain, rather sadly, why it was so easy to work with him, work being yet another safe, distanced level.

She could feel a tender Sam in every stroke he made. Utter devotion to the one thing in the world that mattered to him and in which he could function properly.

'Aspirate for me, please, Tessa.'

She leaned over, calmly using the aspirator to draw fluid and bits from the dog's mouth. But she wasn't calm. She was terribly conscious of him. Of the deep timbre of his voice, of the look those grey eyes gave her above his mask when unavoidably their eyes met.

'Now the amalgam. We'll make sure Juno has a strong occlusal surface for the remainder of her life. She might even be able to enjoy a few marrow bones now.'

Tessa passed the amalgam she had prepared. She watched him smooth and polish the contours of the tooth with those extraordinarily skilled fingers and then check every other, one by one, with painstaking care.

When it was over, he pulled off his mask and gloves and smiled at her. 'Thank you, Tessa. It makes a great difference to have someone working with you who knows what they're doing.'

'There was some advantage in hiring me, then?' she laughed lightly, unhindered now by the worry of how she should react to him. Friday seemed forgotten.

'I — er — suppose I deserved that comment.' His dark eyes held a rueful glint.

'I probably wouldn't have passed it before the op,' she admitted.

He grinned. 'You really are very self-assured for your age, aren't you?'

'Is that approval or criticism?' she enquired.

'Envy, actually,' he laughed.

'How did it go?' Gus interrupted, poking his head around the door.

'Fine. Come in, Gus.'

'How are the other teeth?'

'A couple of borderline cases, but I don't want to keep her under any longer than necessary. We'll see how this goes. She's going to be like a bear with a sore head, knowing Juno.'

Tessa listened as she cleared away, the voices of the two men barely rising above an occasional chuckle. They got on so well. What a pity their futures were in a state of flux when they made such a good team. Gus had several working years in him yet and she knew he admired Sam's youthful energies and new techniques, accepting them as part of growth. Sam on the other hand respected the older man's experience and valued his advice. If only . . .

Tessa stopped herself short. She was organising again. With a shock, she realised Sam was right about her; the format of her upbringing was liable to encroach on almost everything she did, even her work and her ideas about men. The infrastructure of family life was ingrained. It probably meant he was right on that point. Maybe she did like her men to fit into a pattern! Would she unconsciously seek another Archie or Felix or Joe to look after her?

The idea made her run cold! She loved her brothers dearly but she did not want to live with them any more, and, perish the thought, she did not consciously want a lifetime of looking after the same character-type!

Later, thoughtful under the self-analysis that Sam's perceptive comment had triggered off, she began tidying up in the small back room. Stilling her mind, she cleared a way to the word processor, inserted a disc and began the task of documenting Juno's case as a new patient.

She hardly heard Sam walk in and pull out a chair. 'Tessa, have you five minutes to spare? There's something I'd like to talk to you about.'

'Juno?' She flipped her hand over the off-switch and the light of the machine died.

'No, Juno's fine. She won't have a particularly easy time at first, but she'll be OK. No, actually it's about a point I've been discussing with Nina.'

Tessa nodded, turning to him, apprehension in her face.

'You're photogenic — did you know that?' The question was so out of the blue, she stared at him, her eyes astonished.

'Photogenic?' she repeated.

'How do you feel about being on camera?'

She shook her head. 'I don't know. I've never been asked before.'

'You see, you've something special about the way you are . . . I'm not quite sure how to explain it, because I'm only an amateur photographer. But a professional would be able to tell you. Your cheekbones, the structure of your face . . . the way you move . . . I think you'd be just right.'

'Right for what?' She was beginning to feel nervous. In a roundabout way he was coming to something, and she wasn't sure she liked the way he was doing it.

'For a pilot episode of my next television series.'

'But . . . I couldn't act . . . ' she protested. 'Sam, that's silly, are you teasing me?'

'The pilot won't take any acting skills. The more natural the better.'

She couldn't believe he wasn't teasing her. 'Sam, if this is a joke — '

'It's not. I've given the matter a lot of consideration, enough to discuss it with Nina.' He threaded an arm around the back of her chair and a thousand needles danced where his touch connected to her body. The sensation was beginning to terrify her.

'But your programmes are always so full of . . . well, amazingly beautiful women . . . they're so glitzy!'

He nodded begrudgingly. 'Only because I've had to find a way of making them entertaining — in order to snatch the viewers' attention to a very serious subject in a light-hearted way. A documentary with animals has been done umpteen times before and doesn't always increase the ratings, but we've found a successful new formula with veterinary techniques and — for want of a better word — aestheticism.' Aestheticism? Was that what he called beautiful women dripping all over the place?

The feeling of headiness that he had actually conceived her in such a light threatened to swamp her. 'I . . . I don't quite know what to say . . . '

He laughed. 'You haven't heard what I want you to do yet.'

She stared at him. 'What exactly do you mean?'

He was so close that she could see the rough growth of beard which had formed over the day. Her fingers ached to reach up and discover what it felt like, to draw themselves over the strong chin, the full, sensual lips. But what was she doing, thinking like this? She must be quite mad. This was Sam Wilde the television personality talking to her, and she was fully aware of his capacity in that role!

'I've had an idea, you see,' he began persuasively. 'I've suggested to my producer that we do something on the Forest. Bring home a lot of the hazards of the environment. For instance, that pony is representative of hundreds throughout the year. I'd like subtly to bring that point to the fore. We would combine a medical outline incorporating fieldwork with full presentation.'

She knew what full presentation meant. Sam's women lazing seductively across the television screen. But how could he possibly imagine her doing this? 'Has he . . . agreed?' she asked, incredulity in her voice.

'Surprisingly, yes. Just to an initial crew coming down and testing the waters.'

She shook her head. 'I just don't see myself doing that sort of thing, Sam — '

'Oh, no, you've got me wrong! We wouldn't want you as a model or a guest — surely you didn't think that?' he asked scathingly.

She hadn't known what to think, but his scorn at the idea quickly replaced the euphoria of flattery with pink dots of embarrassment in her cheeks.

'I want you for the medical side — to give the programme realism.'

It was like a cold shower of water in her face. She looked into the grey eyes and saw he was serious. 'For . . . the medical side?'

'I want to make the Forest come alive in people's minds. Awaken them to the realities of this particular corner of the British Isles. The dangers as well as the beauty of the place. That's where you would come in — briefly. Perhaps a few minutes in consultation with a client. Gives the whole thing credibility.'

He left her speechless. Not that she was bothered about television, but thinking just for a split-second that he had put her in the same bracket as some of the women she had seen him working with . . .

'Tessa?' An expression of surprised impatience crossed his face and she knew he must be reading her thoughts. 'You didn't think I meant — ?'

'I haven't had time to think at all,' she cut in quickly, hoping his narrowed eyes didn't catch the expression on her face. 'And does it matter what I think? You'll go ahead and do it anyway, won't you?'

'Yes, I probably would,' he answered

without flinching. 'But I'd rather do it with your co-operation than without.'

She turned back to the word processor, the jade slant of her eyes fixed on the screen with determination. 'Then there's no more to be said.'

'You've just typed a double error,' he told her, amusement threading his voice as he watched her fingers glide over the keyboard.

'Thank you.' She just prayed he would go and let her have a breathing space.

When he finally left the room, she sat back in the chair and covered her flushed cheeks with her hands. The incident had underlined for her what intuition had not: that Sam's madness always had a method to it. She wondered what was going on inside that mind of his. Had he witnessed the red streaking of humiliation in her cheeks and neck? Perhaps he had even been intent on causing it.

If he had meant to bring her down to earth, he had certainly succeeded.

* ★ ★

The last few hours dragged. The hands of the clock seemed to be stuck in one position.

She was more than thankful when six came and Sam left to go back to the house. Annie brought a welcome cup of tea into the surgery and the three of them sat down, relaxing in the sliver of a breeze blowing in from the open windows.

The disappointment had dulled. She was just sorry she had let him see it. How stupid of her to think he was asking her to play a glamorous role!

Annie, with her grey hair scooped back into a bun and her friendly smile, sipped quietly as her husband chatted about the day. The older woman seemed to have a sixth sense about Tessa's inner mood, for she drifted the conversation entirely into anecdotes about Gus's days being what she called a vet-of-all-trades.

None of them heard the footsteps on

the porch. And, absorbed in her thoughts, Tessa was the last one to notice the door as it slowly slid open. The look of alarm on Annie's face was what she noticed first.

Gus was quickly on his feet. 'Hello, there!'

Tessa swung around in her chair. She knew at once that it wasn't a client . . . their visitor was hardly from the village. She had sleek chestnut-red hair, coiled behind her ears . . . ears dripping with large, mouth-watering pearls. She wore figure-hugging black and her eyes were cool sapphires.

Gus moved towards her. 'Suzie!' he blustered.

Tessa waited for him to introduce her. But he seemed nervous, and while he was deliberating the red-haired woman walked towards her and held out a hand.

'You must be Tessa . . . Sam has told me all about you.'

Tessa shook hands, puzzled. 'Has he?'

Annie said in a soft voice, 'Tessa, this is Suzie Granger, a friend of Sam's.'

Her brain whirled with images, one of them stilling in her mind. She had seen Suzie Granger before, in an exotic setting, with the fronds of coconut trees swaying in the background set against a tropical sunset. 'I've seen you on television, haven't I?' she asked before she could stop herself. There was no mistaking that gorgeous red hair. 'Sam's last series, wasn't it?'

Suzie Granger released Tessa's hand as sunlight carved shadows across her face revealing a few unkind lines under the exemplary make-up. 'How lovely to be recognised,' she sighed, smiling at Tessa, her eyes glinting ice. 'But it was several series ago, actually.'

'Oh . . . '

Suzie Granger shrugged, a wisp of hair falling from the chignon. 'One can't be lucky enough to get work every time. So much competition nowadays. And . . . you know Sam, don't you?'

Tessa gritted her teeth and forced a token smile. She was beginning to feel that the last person on earth she really did know was Sam Wilde.

4

Suzie Granger turned briefly to Gus. 'Didn't Sam tell you I was arriving?'

'Er — no — he didn't mention it. Are you planning on staying at Beechwood?'

The red-haired woman gave a soft laugh. 'Where else? Beechwood Hall isn't short of space!' She made a dissatisfied clicking sound with her tongue. 'Does one still have to walk up that beastly lane to the Hall? I suppose I shouldn't have let my taxi go, but I thought I'd probably find Samuel here.'

'I'll run you up in the Land Rover,' Gus offered magnanimously, sliding a glance at his wife.

Suzie Granger was already halfway out of the surgery, her well proportioned curves lightly swaying under the svelte black suit, before she looked coolly back at Tessa. The glance was brief, but it could not have said more.

'I'll have to apologise for Suzie,' Annie said after they had gone. 'She tends to think Sam is her own private property and gnashes her teeth at the first hint of competition. But don't let that worry you, she doesn't really mean any harm.'

'She has no competition as far as I'm concerned,' Tessa said coolly, her composure unsettled by the woman's hostile reaction for no apparent reason. 'Is she a regular visitor to Beechwood?'

Annie waved a hand dismissively. 'From time to time. Suzie was a top model five or six years ago, when Sam first started making his series. And she got quite a lot of work then, but modelling is very short-lived. As she said herself, there's a lot of competition these days, especially on television.'

Tessa nodded slowly. 'It's a pity. She's still very attractive.'

The ring of the telephone made them both jump and Tessa got up to answer it. 'Can you speak slower, please? I

94

can't hear you properly,' she pressed, flattening the receiver against her ear trying to make sense out of the woman's distress. 'An accident . . . just past the bridge?' Tessa scribbled down the details on the pad, glancing at the time on her watch and making a mental note. Promising the vet would be along immediately, she replaced the receiver, sighing. 'A hit and run on the main road out of the village. A woman was walking her Alsatian when a car came along and mounted the pavement. Luckily she wasn't harmed but the dog received a direct blow. I'll have to phone Sam.'

'Rotten timing,' Annie sighed.

Tessa nodded, raising her fair eyebrows helplessly. She dialled the number, expecting to hear Greeley, but it was Sam's deep voice which drifted over the line. 'Sam, I'm sorry to trouble you . . . but there's been an accident down by the bridge, a hit and run.'

Sam's voice was abrupt as he responded to the few details. When she got off the phone, she turned to Annie. 'I think it will be Gus who comes.'

'Oh, well, it's understandable. Sam probably has his hands full with Suzie; she's very demanding. I'll leave you to it. I hope it's not too bad, dear.'

Alone, Tessa began to collect together the things she knew would be needed. Slipping a cardigan over her green uniform, shutting the case and with a blanket over her arm, she took one last glance around the surgery, locked up with her set of keys and waited for the rumble of Gus's Land Rover. She was disappointed in Sam's reaction, as though he resented her intrusion into his private life — but what else could she have done?

The Land Rover came almost immediately, trundling like a tractor, the diesel engine groaning to a halt as the passenger door flew open.

'Have we everything there?' a deep voice asked her as she jumped in.

Seeing Sam, she choked back surprise. 'Er — yes, everything . . . '

'Are you OK?'

'Yes, fine.' She drew a long breath, clicking on her safety belt.

'Hold tight, then.' He throttled up to second gear and nearly jerked her head off. 'Just over the bridge, you said?'

'Yes.' Tessa gripped the seat, watching his brown fingers feed the wheel, feeling guilty about her automatic assumption that he would put Suzie before his duty. The deep lines in his face told her just how concerned he was.

'How long has it been since the call?' he asked her.

She looked at her watch. It was almost eight, incredibly. 'Six minutes . . . '

Sam's strong, muscled forearm lashed across the wheel as they turned a corner and half a mile on, as the vehicle ground down in gear, Tessa spotted the bridge.

'Just on the other side,' she directed, 'opposite the cottage. I suppose that's where the woman phoned from.' Her heart started thumping and her pulses raced, the adrenalin flowing liberally through her veins.

Sam swerved the car with a bump on to a grass verge. A small group of people huddled around a shape on the side of the road and as they ran together Tessa heard the disturbing sounds of a woman crying.

'Hello, Jane,' Sam muttered, as they arrived.

The woman, in her late thirties, gazed up with a tearstained face. 'Hello, Sam. Thank God it's you.' She began crying again and an older man and woman tried to comfort her.

Tessa knelt next to Sam and she opened the case for him as he began to examine the Alsatian. There was no doubt that the animal was unconscious, with blood coming from the mouth and nose. She watched tensely as Sam placed his fingers on the lower part of the chest wall on the left side just behind the front leg, trying to find a heartbeat.

His worried grey eyes met hers. 'Just a faint one,' he mouthed to her.

'Can you save him . . . ? Oh, please don't let Bruce die, Sam, please don't!' The woman started sobbing and Tessa put her arm around her shoulders, feeling the stiff, shocked muscles underneath her hand. 'Come on, let's give Sam some air,' she persuaded, glancing at the man. 'Do you live in the cottage?' she asked him.

He nodded. 'We heard the thump. It was terrible. Jane was lucky the lunatic didn't run her over as well.'

'I think it would be a good idea if Jane could go to your cottage with you,' she said gently.

'No!' protested Jane, her voice breaking into fresh sobs. 'I want to be with him.'

'There's nothing you can do.' Sam's voice was firm. 'Go with Mr and Mrs Parker, Jane. Phone Ray from there and get him to come and fetch you.'

Mr Parker took her arm and eased her away from the dog. 'Let Sam handle it. You're only slowing him down.' Eventually she was persuaded to go with the couple to their home.

A few minutes later Bruce lay in the back of the vehicle and Tessa had to keep reminding herself that an unconscious animal could resemble a lifeless one in that there might be no movement for long periods. She mustn't let her negative instincts override her. There was always hope, even though the heartbeat was almost non-existent, but as she crawled in next to him she had the feeling that all they were doing would be of little value in the long run. She could see the same conclusion in Sam's face too, as he closed the doors of the Land Rover.

'Can you manage?' he called back as he threw himself into the front seat.

'Yes, I'm fine.' Looking for the worst of the external bleeding was difficult while trying not to lose her balance. She could feel every bump and hole in the road and at a corner she had to save herself by grabbing hold of the back of Sam's seat.

'Do you want me to stop?' he

shouted, feeling her fingertips brush his shoulders.

She knew he was only asking out of consideration for her and she shouted back as calmly as she could, 'No, it's OK, just drive on.'

She managed to apply a pad of cotton wool to the ear flap like a sandwich, squeezing the part between her fingers and thumb. Her enquiring fingers had already discovered a wound on his side under thick fur and she had done what she could to staunch the flow using special pressure wraps.

When the vehicle finally came to a halt the doors opened and Sam's face appeared, his grey eyes narrowing to a hard sheen as they glanced down at Bruce. She caught hold of the ends of the rug, crouching ready to jump out.

'Can you cope from that angle?' he asked, taking the other ends. She nodded and they bore Bruce in the rug, slung like a hammock between them. He was very heavy, one of the big-boned Alsatians, well fed and cared for. She gritted her teeth and, as Annie had unlocked the door, they carried him in to the first treatment-room.

Sam wrenched off his jacket, already stained badly, and Tessa glanced down, seeing on her own uniform the frightening stain of the animal's life-blood.

It came as no surprise when Sam whispered huskily, 'We're not going to be lucky. He's haemorrhaging inter-nally.'

She filled a syringe, held it as steady as she could and tried to stop trembling as she handed it to him. Her mind lurched back to Jane and the way she had begged Sam to save her dog, but the most terrifying aspect was that a driver could actually damage an animal to this extent, almost kill a person, and then drive off without stopping.

'I'm losing him, damn it, I'm losing him!'

She watched Sam doing all he could and the extent of pain on his face shocked her. He was grey, as though all the energy had seeped into the struggle.

Fifteen minutes later Sam sighed, leaning heavily forward, his hands gripping the table, his head bent. 'No use.' He drew away from Bruce, clenching his fists. When he looked at her, he shook his head. 'Too much internal damage. Bleeding into the chest and abdominal cavities . . . into hollow organs. He's gone.'

Tessa caught her breath in her throat, the implication of the violence sickening her.

'It could have been Jane,' Sam said in a low voice, 'or a child, or any human being walking along that pavement, an innocent bystander. All through the unnecessary speed of one reckless, thoughtless, cowardly bastard!'

She was shocked at his reaction; he seemed to be taking the fatality personally. 'Perhaps Jane will remember the registration — or the model of the car,' she murmured inadequately.

He shook his head. 'I doubt it. It all happened far too quickly.'

'You did everything you could, Sam, everything. He's free of pain. Thank heavens he didn't know what happened to him. And, as you say, Jane is safe.'

His mouth drooped. 'She's going to take this badly. She idolised Bruce. If I had been at the surgery and not up at the house we would have been there quicker . . . '

'It wouldn't have made any difference,' Tessa argued sympathetically. 'You know that. You did all you could. Please don't blame yourself. Jane will understand when she's over the shock. And in time she'll be able to offer another dog a home, a good, loving one.'

He shrugged. 'This is the trouble with getting involved with people, especially in a village or a small community. You feel responsible.'

'It's because you're conscientious that you feel responsible.'

'Still got me down as a man with a vocation?' he asked in a kind of sneer.

'Even more so now,' she answered,

faintly embarrassed.

'I'm angry and I can't do a damn thing about it,' he admitted truthfully.

'I do understand grief,' she said softly; 'it has an insidious way of clouding our perspective for a long time.'

'And my perspective is clouded?' he asked, raising an eyebrow.

'Temporarily. I think you feel responsible for the people in this village ... because they are part of you and you are part of them.'

He sighed, stretching his wide shoulders back and then, with a smile which made the brief intimacy they had shared worth the trouble of words, he drew her outside to the recovery-room, changing the subject in a voice a tone lighter. 'You're right. I've known Jane and Ray for years; they're like an extended family. When I used to come back to Beechwood to see my father Ray would fill me in on all the news and pull my first Forest pint. He's the pub landlord, you see. Bruce here was the pub dog. He was a real character.'

'They're going to miss him,' Tessa agreed quietly.

'Until, as you say, a new Bruce comes along.'

'Maybe a stray who needs a good home or an unwanted pup?'

Sam raised his hand and gently trailed it over her shoulder, his light touch making her shiver. 'Your dress is going to need a good wash.'

'I expect my boss will allow me to claim on expenses,' she answered lightly, trying to look away from the compelling intensity of the grey eyes. She tried also to disregard the hope which blossomed in her heart whenever she caught that look, a hope which budded under the sunny charm of a man like Sam. But in grief charm was tested. She felt in these few brief seconds she had known him as the ordinary man, stripped of his charismatic façade and his professional mask, revealing a vulnerable and sensitive human being beneath.

*　*　*

Jane sat with a cup of tea in her hands in the tiny front room of the cottage.

The Parkers had taken Sam into their garden to inspect the vegetables they were growing and Tessa managed to talk to Jane quietly, pointing out that Bruce had felt no pain after the initial impact. He'd had a long life, full of affection and company, and, though the accident was a dreadful shock, Jane was safe.

'I've phoned Ray,' Jane said eventually, looking through swollen eyes. 'He's getting the bar manager to cover for him and then he's picking me up.' She sipped the sugary tea. 'Ray took it quite well . . . just worried about me, that was all. And I won't repeat what he'd like to do to the driver of that car.'

'He's every right to feel angry,' Tessa consoled. 'But you are the important one. I don't suppose you managed to get a look at the registration number?'

Jane shook her head. She was a

biggish woman with lots of curly brown hair, but at the moment she looked like a lost child. 'No. It all happened too quickly.'

'Sam met with the Forestry Commission people during the week,' Tessa explained, trying to offer some comfort, 'regarding speeding in the village and surrounding areas and perhaps putting more signs up . . . trying to get motorists to cut down their speed.'

'Sam's a campaigner, isn't he?' Jane murmured with a faint smile. 'Just like him to get caught up in the politics of the environment, though I'm sure that doesn't do his television image any good. You can make enemies so easily if you stand up for something.'

'Sam seems to care for the Forest very much,' Tessa agreed softly.

Jane nodded. 'Oh, yes, he does. Not that we see him very often . . . but when we do I always get the feeling this is the real Sam, if you know what I mean. Not the cosmetic Sam of the small screen. You know, the Forest is like a drug.

Take a pinch and you're hooked. We're all hooked. Once you've lived in the Forest you can't live anywhere else; you start caring about the animals and environment passionately.'

With a start, Tessa realised Jane had put into words what was obvious. The villagers seemed to know Sam better than he knew himself. He did care very much. It was too late to distance himself from them, but something within him rebelled, enough to make him drive home the point that he was a television celebrity first and a vet secondly. In the world of television, he didn't have to feel . . . and tonight, when Bruce had died, a little of the veneer had worn away. That was what Sam didn't like. He couldn't cover his emotions.

'We'd better be leaving, Tessa. Ray's coming, isn't he, Jane?' Sam stood with the Parkers, a hint of colour back in his face, but Tessa got the impression that he had been listening and had deliberately intervened before Jane said too much. 'And . . . I really am very sorry I couldn't help Bruce,' he muttered, his lips grimly set.

'You did all you could, Sam, I know that. Thanks for everything you've both done.' Jane's voice was weak, but she managed a grateful smile. 'Nice to have met you, Tessa. I hope I'll see you again.'

On the way home, Sam drove quietly, his concentration centred on the darkened road. Tessa wondered why he had stopped Jane from talking to her. If what she had said was true, he had no reason to be ashamed of his commitment to the Forest. Or was it perhaps his relinquishment of it that pricked his conscience?

Tessa sighed softly and decided she had enough to think about with meeting Suzie back at Beechwood. After the trauma of the day, surely there couldn't possibly be more conflict in store — not tonight, she hoped, crossing her fingers, desperate to sink into bed. It depended, she supposed, on the intimacy of Suzie's relationship with Sam and whether Suzie would regard her as friend or foe.

She glanced at her watch under a sudden shaft of bright moonlight. Twenty minutes to eleven.

'Suzie will be staying for a while,' Sam said, out of the blue, as they turned into the lane and the Porsche crept like a cat to the house. 'I hope you'll get on with her. She means well enough. Try not to take her too seriously.'

Her eyes fluttered open, startled by the words. 'We only met briefly this afternoon . . . Suzie had the advantage of knowing who I was. I was a bit taken by surprise, actually.'

Sam nodded, his profile silhouetted against the darkness. 'Suzie's an old friend. She rang to say she needed a few weeks' breathing space from the modelling work she's been doing. I told her she was welcome to come, that she'd probably get on very well with you.'

Tessa found it hard to imagine Suzie

getting on well with anyone she thought might be standing in her way, especially when it involved Sam Wilde. The icy look Suzie had given her along with the vibes made that quite plain. His plea on Suzie's behalf was natural enough, but it agitated her far more than was reasonable.

'Is Suzie interested in your work?' Tessa asked, trying to ignore the pang of unease.

'That's a funny question. But no . . . she doesn't care for animals much. They shed hair on to clothes, or scuff freshly applied nail polish, that sort of thing. Why?'

Tessa shrugged. 'No reason. It's just that the Forest is an odd choice for a holiday if you aren't keen on its inhabitants.'

'Do I detect disapproval in your tone?'

'No, of course not,' Tessa retaliated quickly. 'I'm sure Suzie will find enough to occupy her.'

'Suzie always does,' Sam answered.

'But I shall still depend on you to provide sympathetic female company.'

Tessa bit her bottom lip, annoyed at herself for making her opinion of Suzie so plain, an opinion which was hardly justified in view of the length of time she had known her.

'I'm sure we shall get along just fine,' she said, trying to convince herself as well as Sam.

When he finally pulled on the brake and the engine died, he sat very still for a moment. Then he leaned across and slowly touched her forehead with his lips. 'Thank you for being such a nice person — and for your support today.'

Tessa ached. She hurt inside until her chest felt like exploding. She was not feeling a nice person, but quite the opposite at the moment. Nasty and spiteful — for no reason at all. And his gentle, friendly kiss made her feel even worse. She could not imagine, in the remotest sense, that he would kiss Suzie Granger like that!

The next she knew he had opened

the door for her and, as she got out, Greeley moved down the flight of stone steps in the darkness like a spectre.

'Miss Granger has retired for the night, sir,' he said softly as he approached.

Sam glanced at her. 'Tessa, you haven't eaten. What can Greeley find you?'

'I don't want any food, thank you, Greeley. I'm all in,' she answered tiredly.

'An early night won't do you any harm,' Sam observed, hunching his shoulders, and they turned towards the house.

Inside, in the cold entrance hall, Greeley disappeared and Sam walked her to the staircase. 'Don't worry if you hear noises outside, it will only be me. I'm going to walk the dogs . . . a midnight therapy.' He half laughed, too apathetically, though, for the humour to contain any real mirth.

Tessa nodded. 'Goodnight, Sam.' She began to climb the flight of stairs, resisting the urge to look back. Why did they feel like Everest tonight? Why did she long for him to call out, Come and walk with me?

But no voice sounded. Why should he want her to walk with him? He'd probably had enough of her company for one day. When she eventually came to the top of the first flight she looked around.

Sam had gone.

The house was in stillness again.

★   ★   ★

Suzie Granger's first words at the breakfast-table next morning were, 'How convenient to have a house guest who also turns out to be a valued member of staff, Sam, darling.' And with a smile that stretched from one bejewelled ear to the other she looked at Tessa and added, 'Forgive me for not realising, Tessa, yesterday. Sam has never been one for details . . . especially important details like who might be living with him.'

'Tessa isn't living with me, Suzie, not in the way your mind works,' Sam told her patiently.

'Oh ... don't mind Sam,' Suzie cooed back. 'He can't take a joke first thing in the morning. No doubt you've noticed breakfasts are a nightmare!'

Tessa folded her napkin and looked at the bubbly, red-headed woman whose make up at eight-thirty was as perfect as she had seen it at seven last night. 'We don't normally eat in here,' she emphasised quickly, 'at least, not breakfast.'

' 'We'?' Suzie repeated slowly, through small white teeth. 'Such a cosy little word, 'we' ... don't you think?' She turned to Sam, her eyes wide.

'I think it's time I wasn't here. I've work to do.' Sam stood up, smiling, raising an eyebrow at his guest. 'No doubt you'll find something to occupy you, Suzie?'

Tessa watched him go, wishing she had never agreed to Greeley's suggestion that he serve breakfast in the Great

Hall. It was a terrible idea. More to the point, why had Sam agreed? Tomorrow she would be safely back in the kitchen with Mrs Pearson!

She edged her chair a few inches from the table and prepared for flight. Suzie, however, anticipated her escape. 'I suppose you and Sam will be closeted together in your little surgery all day?'

Tessa sat still. 'No . . . not all day. Sam and I don't work together in the mornings. If you want him, he'll be with the builders at the rear of the house, I expect.'

Suzie's lips parted in a smile. 'Don't be so defensive, Tessa. Sit and talk with me for a while. It's so deadly boring in this awful mausoleum of Gerry's.'

Tessa reflected on this comment and on her ignorance of the relationship between Sam and the woman sitting opposite. 'Did you know Sam's father?' she asked, her green eyes wide.

'Oh, yes, very well. Sam would bring me up to Beechwood whenever his father was at home.'

'Oh.' She glanced at her watch. She really didn't want to know any more; it was none of her business anyway. Curiosity was a terrible failing and, if she let it get the better of her, no doubt she would open the lid of Pandora's box. Politely she excused herself. 'I'm afraid I'll have to dash. I have to be at the practice for nine to assist Gus.'

'And how did you meet Sam?' Suzie persisted, completely ignoring Tessa's remark.

'I didn't exactly meet him,' Tessa clarified firmly. 'I came for a job interview.'

'Ah . . . yes. Of course, this job of yours! Sam told me the same story.'

'It's quite true,' Tessa defended, feeling rather hot.

'I have to give Sam credit for such novel techniques. But I'm surprised he went to all the bother. He's enough women in his life without having to advertise for one!'

Tessa felt her flesh tighten over her cheekbones. She got up quickly and brushed imaginary crumbs from her clean uniform to cover her fluster. 'I do really have to go now.'

'A pity.' Suzie's attention floated fecklessly to the silver coffee-pot. 'Just when we were getting on so well.'

Realising it was futile to try to talk out Suzie's animosity, Tessa quietly left the room, collected her shoulder-bag and started out for work. The walk was a welcome relief. She couldn't believe trees smelt so delicious. She took deep breaths in through her nose and out through her mouth, slowly, until the air saturated her lungs. It was a beautiful early June morning and everywhere there were fragrant scents. But the sting of Suzie's tongue after last night's bitter failure with Bruce darkened her mood.

When she arrived at the surgery, the small waiting-room was packed out and Gus had already taken a client into one of the treatment-rooms.

Annie had come to help, her arms full with a pretty poodle the colour of sand.

'Sorry I'm late, Annie. I got a little delayed,' she apologised.

'Don't worry. Just take a look at this morning's list and cry hallelujah! It's wonderful the way things are working out!' Annie whispered excitedly. 'People are coming in from all the local areas now. Gerry would have been delighted to see his practice patronised like this.'

Tessa smiled softly, hurrying to help with a dog intent on causing havoc, barking madly. She pushed her more irritating thoughts of Suzie away and decided that, despite what Sam had ordered, staying away from his guest was going to be the only way of avoiding her malice.

'Sorry to hear about Jane's dog,' Annie said, still clutching the poodle. 'She'll be very upset.'

Tessa nodded. 'Sam was too.'

'There have to be one or two he can't help,' said Annie sensibly. 'It would be a perfect world if he could. How about you? You look as though you didn't get much sleep either.'

'Not too bad,' Tessa smiled, gathering her wits and the lead of the hyperactive dog intent on tripping everyone up, burying her face, hoping Annie couldn't read that it wasn't only Bruce who had contributed to her sleepless night.

By the time twelve-thirty came around, Tessa stretched her aching back, walking to the veranda to breathe in the air.

Gus ambled beside her, the door swinging noisily on its hinges behind him. He had removed his white coat and gave a deep sigh of satisfaction. 'Time to stoke the boiler! I'm off for something to eat . . . '

His words trailed off as a car slowed just in front of them. 'That's Suzie in there, isn't it?' he said, frowning.

Tessa squinted her eyes against the sun. She saw Suzie's red head and the pallid face of the man driving the car.

'Who the devil is she with now?' Gus muttered under his breath. 'Whoever it is, they can't be anything but trouble. With Suzie that's a certainty.'

Making no comment, Tessa watched the car disappear. Trouble was an appropriate word. She had sampled some at first hand this morning over breakfast. It was not an experience she would like to repeat.

5

It was at the end of the week, early on Friday morning as Tessa walked to work, that she remembered the remark about trouble.

She saw a host of cameras before she saw Gus.

At first she thought it was the television crew Sam had spoken about, but then she knew by the clamouring and the pushing and shoving that it wasn't.

Gus's warning action came too late. His upstretched arm above the sea of heads caught her attention, but it also precipitated the attention of the reporters. Before she knew what was happening she was surrounded.

The questions came shouted one after another, so fast that she shied away at their intrusiveness and the bodies, which now surrounded her like a thick, breathing wall, pressed in on all sides.

Just as she thought she was about to suffocate, she saw Sam, a head and shoulders above everyone else, barge his way through.

'Don't open your mouth,' he rasped at her, clutching her wrist. Cameras flashed all around them. She was blinded by light. Sam pulled her and she tripped, a reporter standing in her way, knocking shoulders with her.

'Sam, wait . . . ' she began, almost losing her shoe.

'Wait — like hell!'

He yanked her on to the veranda and she saw him turn and with his free hand push a man back. 'Get rid of them, Gus — I don't care how!' he snarled as he propelled her into the surgery, flinging the door closed behind them.

'Are you satisfied?' he fumed, his teeth clenched. 'Are you happy with what you've done?'

'I . . . don't know what you mean!' Tessa stammered, feeling her muscles lock at her shoulder blades.

'You don't? You expect me to believe that?'

Tessa swallowed hard. 'You had better tell me what you're so upset about and perhaps I'll be able to answer your question.'

He picked up a newspaper from the reception desk and bundled it into her hands, his dark eyes accusing. 'Read it!'

Tessa took the paper and gazed, almost unseeing, at an article halfway down the page. A picture of Beechwood Hall caught her eye, then an accompanying paragraph — and her name heading it. Her jaw dropped as she read. When she got to the finish she read it again. 'But . . . this is . . . ridiculous! It says . . . I'm your new . . . '

'Woman — or mistress — or whatever word you used to describe yourself.'

'Me? You think I gave them — '

'What else am I to think? You must have said something! It's all there . . . intimate details of your moving in with me to Beechwood, innuendoes about an affair. How could you do it, you little fool? How could you talk to the Press? I warned you from the very start they would twist things.'

Tessa numbly shook her head. 'But I haven't . . . I really haven't. I just don't know where they got this.'

'Look!' He thrust the paper back under her nose, a brown finger underlining a column she was just too dazed to read. 'The colour of your eyes, your hair, your age, even a reference to an interview . . . who else would have given them those details? OK, they probably distorted what you said, but why speak to them at all? You just had to ignore them, pretend they weren't there if they pestered you . . . or at least come to me.'

'But I didn't say anything, Sam . . . not a thing. I don't know what's going on, really I don't!'

Sam's grey eyes narrowed as if he hardly seemed to hear. 'I'll be damned if I'm going to have my practice turned into a circus by them! I've managed to keep them out up until now — and then you — I should have known!'

'But it isn't me,' implored Tessa. She didn't know what to say to convince him. Whoever it was who had written such lies they had certainly made the worst kind of trouble for her.

'Ignore them from now on!' he growled at her. 'Don't even blink in their direction. They'll misconstrue anything you say. Do you understand me?'

Tessa felt a stab of anger now. The way he was speaking, his unjust and unfair accusations. He hadn't even given her a chance to offer an explanation, but she had such a knot in her throat she could hardly speak, so she merely nodded and turned away from him, clenching her hands.

'I've got the architects coming this morning, of all mornings,' she heard him mutter in a dark voice. 'I'm late already.'

When he had gone, banging the door

behind him, she picked up the paper and tried to read it through blurred eyesight. Tears were on the very verge of falling, but soon she would have to greet clients and it would be no good at all to open the door with red eyes. She dabbed gently at her lashes with a tissue and read a few sentences. Strangely enough, after reading them she felt a little better. Whoever had composed the article had speculated that, since she was living in Beechwood Hall, she was involved in an affair with Samuel Wilde, hinting that she was the current woman in his life. She re-read the article and found herself wondering why Sam had been so angry. So the Press had done their usual embroidering of the truth and jumped to all the wrong conclusions. But did it really matter? If anyone should have been upset, it was she, but a gossip column was the last thing that was going to worry her. What hurt was Sam's accusation and the fact that he hadn't believed her when she'd protested her ignorance of the matter.

She tried hard the rest of the morning to lose herself in her work and not let either Gus or Annie see how distressed she was. She felt slighted and hurt and, for no earthly reason, guilty. And yet she hadn't even seen a reporter before today.

Except perhaps . . .

The thought struck her just after lunch. It was a niggling suspicion at the back of her mind at first, without form or timescale. Then suddenly the memory jumped out at her — the innocuous car and its driver!

But whom could she tell? Whom could she confide in? There had only been one person with her when she'd seen Suzie chauffeured past the surgery — that was Gus! She could hardly involve him. Sam would probably think it was collusion between them anyway, in his present state of mind. And she wasn't sure it was Suzie who had instigated the article — and, even if she was certain, Sam probably would not take her word against Suzie's, judging by the way he'd reacted this morning. Tessa decided she would have to struggle through the day and somehow, later, work out a way to prove her innocence.

★   ★   ★

The boy and girl arrived at the surgery in the afternoon, about ten minutes after Sam. Tessa had to sit them down on the waiting-room bench before she could decipher what the boy was saying. His little sister was crying and too upset to speak.

She gave the girl a peppermint from her pocket, usually kept for bribery of a recalcitrant animal, then she offered one to the boy, who told her his name was David.

'Tell me what's wrong, David, as slowly as you can, and we'll see what we can do to help.' The boy was about eight, Tessa thought, his sister six or seven. She settled on her knees, her hands knitted in with the children's and asked him to begin his story again.

'There's a pony by the brook,' he told her, sucking furiously on the peppermint. 'She's rolled on her side and she's making funny noises.'

'She's not just sleeping or having a lie-down?' Tessa asked gently.

He shook his head. 'She kicked out at Millie.'

Tessa smiled down at the girl who nodded, her eyes dried with dirt and tears under the lashes. 'Star never kicks. But she did just now.'

'Star? You know her, then?' Tessa waited while they looked at each other and obviously by silent mutual consent agreed on the answer. 'She's our pony,' Millie whispered with half a smile and half a sigh. 'Me and my brother's.'

'You mean . . . you own her? Your mummy and daddy own Star?'

Confusingly, David and Millie shook their heads. Millie began to cry and David looked at Tessa with soft brown eyes and said, 'She's not exactly ours. But she's ill, we know she is.'

131

Tessa tightened her grip on the damp little hands and smiled. 'Does your mum know you're here?'

'No. But will you come to see Star — please?' David wriggled himself off the seat and his little sister scrambled up beside him.

'We'll come,' said a voice from the back of the room. They turned and saw a very tall, curly-headed man with a wide smile which was just a little bit crooked.

Tessa looked at Sam nervously. He appeared to have calmed down after the morning's outburst and his eyes were a soft, clear grey, the dark pupils sprayed with tiny flecks of silver and yellow.

'Can you take us to Star?' he asked, patiently bending down on his haunches. Tessa let her gaze linger over the strong, broad shoulders covered in red check cloth. His hair, the colour of burnished conkers, curled in thick twists over his collar and her heart did an immense leap as her eyes wilfully lingered. Returning to the present with difficulty, she heard the children giving directions.

'Would you like a ride in a Land Rover?' he asked them, standing up.

David and Millie nodded, their cheeks ablaze with colour.

'Tessa, would you ask Gus if he'd mind us borrowing the Land Rover? And would he keep an eye on the surgery? I'll collect what we need . . . oh, yes, we'd better give Mrs Dockens a ring and tell her the children are here. In fact we must get her permission to take them with us to find the pony.'

'Do you want me to phone her?' Tessa asked, feeling Millie's tiny, sticky hand slip into hers.

'Five-ow-free-four,' Millie sang beside her and Tessa looked down and laughed softly.

'Looks as if you've got the job,' Sam said. 'Mrs Dockens' husband works for the Forestry Commission so I'm sure she'll understand.'

'You know the family?' she asked, surprised.

'I know Mrs Dockens well enough to guarantee you she'd have a fit if she thought the kids had gone out of bounds,' he told her, casting a frown at the two dirty faces.

Tessa walked hand in hand with Millie to the telephone, rejoicing in the fact that Sam had spoken without rancour — or was it just that he was so preoccupied with the children he'd forgotten his anger with her?

Lifting Millie up to the phone on her hip, Tessa had a three-way conversation with Mrs Dockens, who eventually agreed to her children going with them. Millie's mum explained that Star was a regular visitor to their cottage — sometimes stopping the traffic, refusing to budge. Only the children, apparently, had the technique of coaxing her out of harm's way.

A few minutes later Tessa was sitting beside Sam in the Land Rover and the children excitedly pointed directions from the back seats. The bumpy terrain led into secluded dark green woodland, ferns and bracken growing waist-high.

'You don't often come out here by yourselves, do you?' Tessa asked, appalled at the thought that the children had been here alone with the pony.

'We had to follow her,' David said in a small voice.

''Cos she was acting funny,' added Millie, holding on for dear life to the back of Tessa's seat as they lurched across a ridge of turf.

'And you came straight to the surgery when she went on her side . . . when she kicked?' Sam persuaded gently as he drove, frowning into the distance.

'We ran all the way,' David answered, his eyes scanning the windscreen. 'Look . . . there she is . . . by the stream.'

Sam flung the Land Rover to a halt and they all clambered out. Tessa found Millie in her arms, crying quietly, 'Star's dead, I know she's dead.'

And Tessa was inclined to think the

same. The pony looked motionless on her side, stretched in a peculiar position, her body twisted.

Sam snatched his case from the back and then said to the children, 'Both of you wait here, in the Land Rover. Don't touch anything.'

Tessa gently put Millie down and kissed her forehead, then she squeezed David's hand. 'We won't be long. Do as Sam says, won't you? David, I'll leave you in charge.'

It was obvious when they got near to the pony she was not dead, but she was having difficulty with her breathing and guttural choking sounds were coming from her mouth. She made no attempt to move as they drew near, and Sam put up a warning hand.

'Tessa, I've got a hunch. If we need to give her a sedative we will, but I don't think there's time. If you could try to soothe her, call her by name, I'm going to examine her mouth. I've a feeling I know what's wrong. But, whatever you do, keep out of reach of those legs, because they could send you flying.'

Tessa nodded. She avoided all four limbs, knelt by Star's head and began to stroke her very gently. But as Sam closed his fingers around her jaws the pony made an attempt to right herself, her powerful neck lifting from the ground and knocking Tessa back with a thump. Winded and on her side, she felt Sam's strong arms quickly around her.

'Tessa! Are you hurt?' He sat her up, his hands gently under her armpits. It was all she could do to get her breath back.

'I . . . I'm fine . . . ' She felt nauseated but she smiled. 'Really I am. Try again, Sam, please.'

He held on to her as she got back to her knees, but she slid his hands away, encouraging him towards the pony. 'Please, Sam . . . I'm not hurt; see to Star.'

Reluctantly he moved back again to the pony's mouth. Tessa shook the muzziness from her head, reaching out to lay her fingers on the roughly matted coat. The pony did not stir this time and she shifted a little closer, despite the sensation of just having collided with a brick wall.

'Are you sure you want to go ahead with this?' Sam asked, eyeing her with concern.

'Yes . . . of course!' She turned her gaze down and felt a sharp pang of pity. The whites of the pony's eyes were so white they gleamed like crescent moons. 'Hurry, Sam!'

He gave a nod and a fleeting encouraging smile, then with strong hands he eased apart the pony's jaw. As she whispered softly to Star she watched him probe into her mouth gently, using forceps. Several tries later, he shifted his position. 'Almost there, hang on.'

Her blood rushed noisily in her ears as the tension made seconds seem like hours.

'Here we are . . . ' he breathed, relief tinging his voice.

'What is it?'

'A piece of plastic bag, I'm afraid. Star must have sniffed food in it and sucked it into her windpipe.'

'Do you think you've got all of it?'

He nodded, the pony unwilling to be touched any longer. 'If I've retrieved it all, she'll be up in no time, so be prepared, Tessa. Move back now.'

She rose and moved a few feet back into the clearing. Sam hardly had time to get out of the way himself and he was forced to abandon his equipment as Star struggled to her feet.

'Oh, Sam ... she's going to be all right! But how did you know? she gasped in amazement.

'I've treated suffocation before — and haven't been so lucky either, because I've been called out too late or no one had spotted the animal in distress.'

'Do you think it was rubbish she picked up?'

'Unfortunately yes. If it isn't plastic bags, it's tin or bottle-tops or string entangled around their intestines. Litter is a curse. Star was just lucky she had such diligent friends in the children.'

The pony shook and raised her head, arching her neck. Sam said, 'No coughing . . . good.' He watched her move around. When he was satisfied with her recovery Tessa watched him grab his case and deposit the evidence of the injury into a small transparent holder.

'There's no chance of her having any more debris in her windpipe?' Tessa asked uncertainly.

'I think I cleared the obstruction,' Sam frowned. 'Unless I have her under anaesthetic I can't do much more. And I would have to turn the matter over to the Forestry Commission in that case. She's looking pretty good, but I'll keep an eye on her all the same.'

As Star moved away, already beginning to graze, Sam collected the rest of his equipment. 'I was more worried about you,' he said as she bent to help him.

Her skin seemed to leap at his

concern. She had forgotten the knock now. She smiled at him, her mind a blank for the moment.

'Star!' The children were calling from the Land Rover.

'We'd better go and tell them what happened,' he said, grinning. 'They'll want to know all the gory details. Kids always do.'

She walked alongside him, aware of his easy-moving body, which reminded her what a deceptive mortal he was with his lethargic grace.

Millie and David jumped from the Land Rover and came running into their arms. 'Is she better? What did you do to her?' As Sam said, the children wanted to know all the details, gruesome ones especially, and he patiently leaned on the bonnet, explaining what had happened.

Eventually, satiated with knowledge, Millie held out her plump arms and Tessa hoisted her on to her hip. Her little eyelids fluttered and she gave a great yawn.

'Someone's tired,' Sam laughed.

'I'm not,' David protested. 'Can we just go over and say goodbye before we go?'

Tessa felt a stir on her shoulder. 'You two go,' she whispered. 'I'll get in and sit with Millie at the back.'

Sam grinned. 'OK. We won't go too close.'

He moved without haste, hands in pockets, accompanied by the small figure of David, down to the stream to watch Star drink. Tessa climbed aboard and relaxed in the back seat where she had a good view of the two of them, Millie curled snuggly in her lap. Having the tiny body so close and dependent made her shiver inside with pleasure. The soft rise and fall of the child's even breathing mingled with her own. From the window, she could see the two figures, Sam leaning against the tree, his hand on David's small shoulder, the boy looking up at him, his face catching the sunlight. A peace spread over the glade, just the sound of birds at treetop distance beginning their late afternoon chorus.

When they clambered back into the vehicle, David sat in the front seat, his face flushed with excitement. 'Millie's all right, isn't she?' he asked, casting a responsible eye over his sleeping sister.

'She's pretty exhausted,' Tessa smiled. 'I expect it was all the running she's done.'

David grinned and looked back at Sam. 'We saved Star, didn't we?'

Sam nodded as he started the engine. 'You most certainly did.'

'Will you tell Mum that? She doesn't like us going off, 'specially Millie.'

Sam chuckled. 'Don't worry. I'll explain everything.' Tessa studied their heads, almost identical in colouring, a goldeny brown as the light flooded in, but the boy's hair was straight as a die and Sam's curled thickly.

David's eyes never left Sam for a moment as he registered every word, watching him control the Land Rover. Sam spoke gently and laughed a lot and every now and then caught her gaze in the driving mirror.

Millie meanwhile was a warm little body cradled in her arms, her thumb wedged in her mouth and a crumpled handkerchief in her hand which she called her 'silkie'.

The Land Rover kangarooed over holes and jangled across cattle grids and a deep ditch where the wheels burned the ground, made them all go 'oooh' as the engine churned like a jet plane.

Eventually they came to a halt outside a pretty cottage covered in vine, its white and pink flowers frosting the walls and windowsills. She found herself staring into the face of a woman whom Sam must know well, for she was smiling up at him, one hard-working hand resting on his forearm.

Mrs Dockens shook her head at her daughter in Tessa's arms. 'Up to more mischief, I suppose?'

Tessa grinned and felt Sam's arms curl around her to help her out. 'No,

Mrs Dockens, quite the opposite.'

'Bless you both, I was about to call their dad when you phoned,' she sighed, shaking her head despairingly, taking a sleeping Millie into her arms. Turning to David, she gave his shoulder a playful shake. 'Next time you go chasing ponies, you come in and tell me first! I thought you were buying ice-creams at the shop!' she frowned.

'It was our fault, keeping them until this hour,' Sam apologised. 'If it weren't for David and Millie, Star would have choked to death. Worth an extra half an hour up before bedtime tonight perhaps?'

Mrs Dockens grinned. 'P'raps. We'll have to see what their dad says. That pony! It's a wonder they don't bring her in to eat from the table. She's not ours, you know. Anyone would think she was. She's got her head over the garden fence at six in the morning!'

Sam laughed, then gathered a relieved-looking David on his strong shoulders and gave him a ride to the cottage. Tessa watched from the Land Rover. She wanted to see everything, scrutinise all Sam's movements, listen to the faint murmurings of his voice . . . unnoticed. She wanted it all, every little detail.

★   ★   ★

'Doesn't Star have a real owner, one who could check up on her more frequently?' Tessa asked, settling herself in the front seat. They were on their way home now, the two children safely deposited, the warmth of Sam's body next to hers making her give a little shudder of pleasure.

He drove carefully, back on to the main road. 'Oh, yes, she has an owner. The ponies are branded by law. Each commoner has his own symbol or sign. Horses are branded at the annual drift, usually on the shoulder, as Star has been, though you probably didn't notice. Brands are essential in identifying animals involved in accidents.'

Tessa looked shocked. 'The brand

still didn't stop her from nearly suffocating!'

'And David and Millie's parents, ever watchful and responsible as they are, didn't stop their children from winding up in the Forest — miles from anywhere!'

'I know,' Tessa agreed ponderously, 'but as far as letting animals loose surely there must be a better system?'

'If you can think of one I'm sure the Forestry Commission would be very pleased to hear about it.'

She shrugged, darting a look at him. 'Letting the animals roam . . . it just seems so risky . . . '

'The Forest can be a risky place. But it's not a prison or a zoo. It's a sanctuary and a haven. Life has its paradoxes here — and we know enough about the extremes in this profession, don't we? It's just not possible to compartmentalise nature; you have to take the rough with the smooth, do the best you can.'

She gave a deep sigh. 'I hope Star will

be OK — for the children's sake.'

He chuckled, his eyes creasing. 'Stop worrying. I'll check her tomorrow — for the children's sake — and for yours.'

They drove in silence for a while. Tessa was lulled by the consistent drone of the engine and her lids crept closer to her cheeks in lethargy, but her sense of well-being was suddenly shattered as Sam braked hard and cursed, his whole body stiffening.

'They're back, damn it!' He swerved the Land Rover left, into the courtyard of the Crossed Keys.

Tessa clung on to the seat, watching the bull nose of the vehicle come to a halt just before it collided with a patio full of white plastic chairs and umbrellas.

'W-what's the matter?' she stammered, roughly thrown out of her sleepiness.

'Didn't you see? Outside the practice?'

She knew without him having to tell

her. 'It was the reporters again, wasn't it?' she mumbled, colour flaring in her cheeks — as if she had done something wrong.

Sam cursed under his breath, driving his fist on to the edge of the steering-wheel. 'I thought we had got rid of them!'

Tessa sat with her eyes in her lap and her pulse pounding in her ears. What could she do? What could she say? If she persisted in protesting her innocence, he would just become more angry, she could sense it. And yet none of this was her doing!

She was relieved to see Jane hurrying from the rear door of the Crossed Keys, one friendly face at least. 'Sam . . . Tessa . . . ' she called. 'Come on in, we're just opening up.'

His eyes were diamond-hard. She could physically feel his hostile vibrations. Poor Jane wasn't going to get a welcome reception. But to her surprise he made an effort to smile. 'We'd like to, Jane, but perhaps another time.

Unfortunately we've a few problems.'

Jane gave a wry grin and pulled open Tessa's door. 'You're telling me? The pub was packed with them at lunchtime.'

Sam ground his teeth. 'Stupid of me. I might have known.'

Jane shrugged dismissively. 'They'll get fed up with hanging around tomorrow — or the next day. Then things will go back to normal. You should know, you've had media attention before, Sam.'

He nodded grimly. 'Which is why I want to avoid any more!'

Tessa turned to him, her full mouth open in protest. She wasn't the cause! Why wouldn't he believe her? He was being so unfair!

'Come into the kitchen garden and let me make you a long cool drink and some sandwiches,' Jane persisted. 'You both look as though you could do with sustenance. Going over to the surgery is only going to start them off again. Gus and Annie will handle it.'

After a brief hesitation Sam nodded his agreement. 'Tessa had a brush with a pony earlier,' he said as he jumped out from the Land Rover. 'It was a real thump. I'm sure a drink and a bite to eat would help.'

Tessa glanced at Jane as she stood there, conscious of her rumpled green uniform and dust over her slip-on shoes.

'Come on, then,' beckoned Jane. 'I'll take you to safety.'

As she followed Jane into the flat at the back of the pub and out again into the kitchen garden, filled with shrubs and summer flowers, Tessa felt slightly appeased. Sam, even in his anger, had been thoughtful of her. If only those reporters hadn't shown up again.

'Make yourselves comfy on the lounger,' Jane offered. 'No one is going to bother you out here. It's our little desert island.'

The lounger turned out to be a long floral-covered swing seat, padded and canopied, surrounded by tubs of geraniums and fuchsias and sheltered by a thick red brick wall. Tessa watched Sam spread himself on to the seat, his large body denting the thick cushions, his arm flung across the back. 'I won't bite.' He gestured to the vacant space next to him.

She sat down, her long hair falling from the ribbon into which she had tied it for work. The ribbon dropped on to the seat and Sam's brown fingers picked it up abstractedly as she sat beside him.

Hating the empty silence, she turned to him. 'Sam . . . it really wasn't me who — '

'You can't go back to Beechwood tonight,' he interrupted calmly. 'More of them will be up at the house.'

She stared at him, her green eyes bright in alarm. Her heart was flitting around inside her like a bird. 'But does it matter, Sam? What more can they do? I really don't understand why you're so upset about them printing that rubbish — '

'Because that's precisely what it is. Rubbish. People are taken in by it . . . believe the worst . . . do you really want them to think you are 'imported' to Beechwood just for my enjoyment?'

She saw he was deadly serious. He was more concerned for her reputation than she was. 'But you and I know that isn't true,' she protested. 'What does it matter about people who are foolish enough to believe lies?'

He stared at her, his mouth in a straight line, opening in a slight gasp. 'It matters a great deal! Because it won't just stop there; once they scent a story, they follow it doggedly to its bitter end and they take you with it.'

She shook her head, not understanding his reaction. 'But is what people think important? Is it a big enough issue to worry over like this?'

'Obviously not to you! But it worries the hell out of me. And at the moment I just can't add another responsibility to my work schedule.'

'Your . . . work schedule?' Her green

eyes narrowed to cat-like slits of comprehension.

'You shouldn't have started the ball rolling in the first place,' he had the audacity to inform her.

'But I didn't! Why won't you believe me?' she cried, exasperated.

'This is ridiculous, Tessa. I don't want to lose you, but . . . ' He sighed deeply, rubbing brown fingers over his chin. 'As far as I can see, there is only one alternative. If you weren't here, they would go away, as Jane says.'

'If I weren't here?'

His gaze was cold grey as he stared back at her. 'I'm sending you away from Beechwood for a while. You haven't had time off. I think a few days is appropriate.'

The smooth-skinned curve of her cheek began to twitch under the downy pale hairs that showered her face. 'But I've nowhere to go!'

Sam frowned impatiently. 'Of course you have. You can go home to Oxford. Your family will want an explanation.

They're bound to have read the newspapers. No finer time than now to give them one. And if you're not here, Gus and Annie won't have to worry about covering up for you.'

And neither will you, she thought with annoyed disappointment. You just want to get rid of me, Sam Wilde. I'm in the way. I'm a hindrance. You wish you'd never hired me. She turned to look at him, tight-lipped — it didn't matter to him that she was unbearably hurt and humiliated.

'Don't look at me like that, Tessa. You can't always have your own way. You may think you're experienced enough to handle the situation here but you will have to take it from me that you're not.'

She bit her bottom lip, averting her eyes, wishing fervently that she had never got up on that Saturday morning, never attended the ill-fated job interview. Ever since then her life had been turned upside-down by this man!

He was treating her like a parcel, packing her off and out of his life, and she had done nothing to warrant such treatment. Unless, of course, he wanted to be alone with Suzie . . .

Her worst fears crystallised as he said, without raising his voice above a whisper, 'I'm going to put you on the train this evening. I'm sorry, Tessa, but I see no alternative. You'll have to go.'

6

The train slipped slowly out of the station.

Tessa pressed her nose against the window and stared along the empty platform, her eyes wide.

Sam's tall figure had gone.

Her body went slack in the seat as the train gathered speed but her thoughts were still at the Crossed Keys. How could he just pack her off like this?

She laid her head back on the seat remembering the afternoon. Watching him engrossed in conversation with David, studying his thick brown tousled hair and his strongly defined masculine features, the slight lean of his head to one side as he listened to the boy, had made her feel warm and secure inside. But how could she feel like this about a man who treated her so badly the next minute?

The train grumbled into Oxford at dusk. She hailed a taxi, watched the red- and yellow-streaked sky turn to ebony and, amid a sinking, empty feeling, considered her next problem. Telling the family.

'Just here, thank you.' Tessa leaned forward, banishing the thought of Beechwood from her mind, and pointed to her house, ablaze with lights.

She paid the fare and watched the taxi disappear. Her tummy arched at the familiar sight and sounds of the tidy, organised town-house.

'Tessa!' A crack of golden light escaped from the front door. Suddenly there was Felix, Todd and Archie and her father spilling out on to the lawn.

'Welcome home, darling,' Joe said, his eyes bright.

'You knew . . . ?' she mouthed, staring at them in surprise.

'Your boss just phoned,' her father explained. 'We were flipping a coin to see who would come and meet you from the station.'

Tessa considered the four pairs of eager eyes. She had to smile. They were bursting to ask questions and not making a very good job of containing themselves. She stared up at her father. 'Oh, Dad!' she mumbled, a tiny, hidden sob running through her body as he turned her face into his shoulder and almost squeezed the life out of her as they walked into the house.

* * *

'Why don't you want to come out, Tessa? It's a beautiful evening. You've spent all weekend indoors.'

Tessa picked at the hem of her cut-off shorts. She and Todd were sitting in the garden. He was like a great golden Labrador with his buttery tan and white-blond hair. But every time she looked at him she saw another face and she couldn't help it. The superimposing of Sam was like a spell. His grey eyes, glimmering in Todd's blue ones, his chestnut curls twisting in disorder covering Todd's blond mane. She blinked ferociously and stood up, forcing herself to concentrate. She would go mad if she moped around the house any longer. Not a word from Sam. Three days of utter silence!

'You'll come?'

'I'll come,' Tessa agreed, forming her full mouth into a reticent smile.

The party turned out to be fun, young people enjoying themselves. For a Monday evening, it took away the miserable air of the beginning of the week. Todd introduced her to his friends, new ones she hadn't met before, and she began to let the tension unwind from her body. It was only when a young girl called Amber with soft brown hair and hazel eyes came over and began to talk to her about the newspaper article that she felt her nerves knit.

'You shouldn't believe all you read in the newspapers,' she told her, seeing the same look of disbelief on her face as she'd seen on her brothers' when she'd tried to explain about the article. Sam was right — again. People didn't want to know the truth.

'You're so lucky, working for a man like that,' Amber said with admiration.

Tessa crunched her teeth on a savoury biscuit — hard! 'Mmm,' she muttered under her breath and then smiled repentantly when the girl looked at her, puzzled.

It was difficult to get off the subject of Sam Wilde. Pleading a headache, she decided, was going to be the line of least resistance. She would have caught a taxi home and been happy with a few minutes to get her breath back, but Todd shook his head fiercely. 'There's a blues night on Thursday,' he told her as he drove. 'And I won't take no for an answer; headaches don't last that long!'

Tessa took an inward breath and suddenly realised she had no reason to refuse. She wasn't going anywhere. It was obvious Sam had no intention of phoning.

The next few days passed painfully

slowly. Joe's gaze met hers with a look which said he cared, but diplomatically he left her to her own devices and disappeared with the twins to work.

She peered out from the window on a rainy Thursday afternoon and contemplated the emerald lawns and the neat brick walls of the houses. A far cry from the Forest where the landscape would be in a state of glorious chaos.

She missed it so much.

She could taste the salty pine on her lips, smell the leaf mould and the bark, hear the chorus of bird noises which filled twilight and dawn with a throbbing intensity. She could see Beechwood Hall in her mind's eye; Greeley and Mrs Pearson and her village gossip and the builders and their problems . . . hear Sam's stubborn refusal to commit himself to the architect's suggestions . . . The memories tumbled back.

A rosy sun broke through the clouds.

The summer afternoon burst out with golden shafts of light. It was her undoing, thinking like this, she decided, suddenly angry with herself. She might as well accept the fact that Sam had eased her out of his life, very cleverly.

She must pull herself together and start making something of her own!

* * *

'Having a good time?' Todd shouted above the music.

'Great!' Tessa moved with the rhythm, her slender body swaying, her hair loose over her back. She wore a long gypsy skirt and a broderie anglaise blouse, her body tingling and supple as it touched the material.

Todd and his friends were nice people, she'd discovered, especially Amber, the girl with light brown hair and pretty eyes who had asked about Sam. Luckily the topic hadn't come up again.

She had actually been driven by the sheer force of sound to think only of listening and moving to the beat. But when the groups began to pack away, Todd's fingers wrapped around her waist and he shouted, 'Come on, there'll be a mad dash in a moment!'

Luckily they were the first out, and Todd drove the sports car into the empty streets of Oxford without having to queue from the car park.

'Where to now?' he asked her, grinning.

'Home, James. I'm exhausted.'

'You're out of practice,' he laughed, but with a shrug added, 'Are you going to invite me in for a nightcap?'

She gazed at the sky, full of little gems, the wind cool against her hot skin, then laughed at Todd's mischievous grin. 'At least I can just push you over the fence if you make a nuisance of yourself!'

Tessa had her key in her hand as they walked the path to her house. They were still laughing softly as the door opened. Joe Dance stood there, his shirt-sleeves rolled up. 'Have a good time, you two?'

'Fantastic,' Todd answered, his eyes catching Tessa's uncertainly.

'Stay for a coffee,' Joe offered.

Tessa watched as Todd, with a relieved glance in her direction, strolled in. She decided to freshen up and brush her hair, so it was five minutes before she reappeared, opening the lounge door, her eyes bright and her face fresh under a dab of moisturising cream.

'Dad, have you put the coffee — ?' Tessa felt the energy run so fast from her body that she thought she was going to faint.

The man in the armchair stared across at her. His eyes were dark and forbidding. His body was taut, tightly muscled under jeans and the large, hair-covered forearms heaved the long body upwards, so that her lips parted in a gasp. 'Sam!'

'Hello, Tessa.'

The silence dragged between them until Joe spoke. 'Mr Wilde — er — Sam arrived just after you two left. We've — er — '

'Drunk tea,' supplied Sam.

'And talked,' added her father.

She managed to smile, her lips trembling. Then she was aware of Todd beside her, his fingers touching her arm. The smile he gave almost convinced her it was genuine, but the tension in the room was so electric she knew he was only trying to be polite. 'My turn for a raincheck this time,' he said softly.

He swerved his attention back to the other two men and nodded in Sam's direction, a distinct coolness between the two men. She could feel their eye-contact and she wasn't surprised when Todd said, 'I'll have that coffee another time, Mr Dance. See you tomorrow, Tessa.'

Her pulses were far too rapid as they walked to the front door. 'Todd . . . I'm really sorry . . . '

'Don't be. It's not your fault he was here,' he said grimly. 'If you want me, you know where I am.'

She watched him take the fence, his

long legs propelling him athletically over. She stood for a moment feeling her body shake, wondering why she felt as though she was going back to face a firing squad.

Walking into the room, she saw Sam's expression, which had no friendliness in it. Her heart took a sideways dive.

'I'm going to leave you two to have a good chin-wag,' her father said. 'Past my bedtime. And . . . Tessa, Sam's staying in the spare bedroom. Not much fun in driving back to Hampshire in the middle of the night, is there?'

She glanced affectionately at her father and nodded. But she couldn't understand why Sam was here at this time of night, or why he had even bothered to come after a week's silence. 'Goodnight, Dad,' she said hesitantly, and kissed him on his cheek as he went out.

When the door closed, she looked back to Sam, sticking out her chin and drawing back her shoulders. Before tonight she would have done practically anything to be in his company again. But over the week she had gradually come to terms with the fact that he didn't want her in his life. She complicated his affairs, and Sam Wilde wasn't prepared for any complications to his existence. She had come to much the same conclusion herself, having been given time to think things out, and she did not want him around now, upsetting the fragile resolutions which she had just begun to make about her own future.

'Did you drive? I didn't see your car?' she asked, cool courtesy finding her voice.

'Your father suggested I park it in the garage overnight.'

'Have you had coffee?'

'Tea — and a couple of beers. Your father is a good host.'

She took the innuendo . . . that she hadn't been there to offer one herself. But all of a sudden she felt too ragged to be polite. 'Why have you come, Sam?'

He got up, his long legs hard and muscled under the fabric of his jeans. The navy blue cord shirt tugged at the skin underneath, his tan so deep that even the tendrils of chest hair winding up to his throat seemed lost in it. She seemed to know every inch of that body. Had she spent so many hours just watching him?

'Why do you think I've come?'

'I don't honestly know. I assumed your silence indicated you didn't want to know any more. That my job was over.'

'Do you want it to be over?'

He wasn't putting himself out to help at all. In his manner there was no tang of regret or apology for the anxiety he'd caused her. Did he recognise anything except his own selfish motives?

'I think I ought to tell you that I — '

'That you don't want to come back with me?' he cut in sharply, his eyes narrowing.

Tessa caught back a little gasp, her fair eyebrows pleating together. 'To come back with you? But I don't understand . . . '

'Or you don't want to understand. You seemed to be enjoying yourself far too much tonight to be giving the matter of your job much thought.'

Now he was trying to make it seem as though a week's silence were her fault! 'Yes, I was enjoying myself,' she admitted calmly, the faintest pink flush tinging her cheeks. 'Did you expect me to stay in by the phone, guarding it?'

'I expected you to be here, at least.'

'Then why not ring first?' she asked, trying not let the tone of annoyance raise in her voice.

'And make an appointment, I suppose?' Sam retaliated, with pointed sarcasm.

Tessa's jaw slackened in shock. It was as though he was accusing her of something devious! Surely he hadn't any right to comment at all? Not a single word from him in days and he was taking this attitude!

She was very angry now, so angry she

was having difficulty in keeping her temper under control. 'Did you expect me to wait around — like everyone else?' she asked shakily. 'You think the world revolves around you but it doesn't. At least, I don't!'

He leaned back on his heels, surveying her, his eyes glimmering like ripe olives. 'I thought the job might have meant more to you than this,' he said slowly. 'If you care to remember, my advertisement specified flexibility. You knew what you were getting yourself into when you took the job. I warned you, you can't deny that. Now you're whining because I haven't stuck to a timetable. If you were so damn worried about not hearing, why couldn't you have phoned me?'

She gave a little gasp. 'Yes, I do understand now! You've come because you're curious, aren't you? Because your pride has been hurt. You expected me to phone you! You wanted me to chase after you, and my job — that's at the bottom of it, isn't it?'

'Don't be so ridiculous, Tessa!'

She hadn't realised he'd been creeping up on her, his large body moving with stealth across the floor. They were breathing hot air at one another. He gripped her wrist as she went to move away and she found herself caught, all the resentment of the last few days boiling up in her.

'I did you the biggest favour of your life getting you out of Beechwood Bridge, don't you realise that? Then I drive here to collect you and I find you sneaking through your own front door at God knows what hour,' he grated.

Tessa wrenched back, but he held firmly on. 'You've got a nerve, Sam, you really have,' she whispered hoarsely, hoping her father couldn't hear what was going on. 'Don't think you can treat me like one of your women, because you can't!'

He glared at her, his fingers hurting her skin. 'I couldn't agree more! It's precisely because I was concerned for your reputation — that you wouldn't be labelled as one of 'my women' as you put it — that I did what I did.'

'But you over-reacted! And you are over-reacting now — you're hurting me!'

Stunned by her remark, he let go of her, his fingers leaving red patches on her wrist. He stood indecisively, frowning at them. 'Tessa . . . I'm sorry . . . what the hell are we doing arguing like this?'

'I'm not arguing, Sam.'

He picked up her arm, held it gently between his fingers and massaged the red spots. When they had evaporated, he looked at her with such regret that all her resolutions disappeared into thin air. Don't look at me like that, Sam Wilde, she prayed, don't!

'Well?' His eyebrows quirked up questioningly, his body warmth coming over in great waves. 'What are we going to do about the situation?'

She tugged away her arm, the emotional blackmail of those grey eyes too formidable to withstand.

'I didn't mean to hurt you,' he said, quietly regarding her.

He hadn't hurt her. Inside she ached, perhaps. But she couldn't even begin to work her feelings out for herself, let alone discuss it rationally with him. There came a moment of intense awareness between them, every nerve-end in her body reacting to him. There was an undercurrent which made her flesh burn.

'Tessa ... ' He turned slowly, the back of his dark head bent down. 'Words are supposed to be the best form of communication — ' his voice cracked tensely ' — but they seem to be our worst enemy sometimes.' He looked up, eyeing her strangely. 'What I'm trying to put into words ... is ... and I'm doing a very poor job of it ... I want you back. I need you at Beechwood.'

She could not believe it. Her heart virtually stopped. He was the only man who had ever made her feel like this — furious one moment, achingly tender the next, wanting to run to him, to put her arms around him . . .

She already knew the answer when he asked, 'Will you come back to the Forest with me? Will you?'

★ ★ ★

The golden retriever was a beautiful dog.

Gus said, 'Well, what do you think? Surgery?'

Sam nodded. 'Yes, I suppose so. She's already had too much pain with that stifle rupture. Has she eaten?'

'Not a thing.'

Sam stroked the wide, ruffled golden head. Large, thick-fringed brown eyes watched his every movement. 'Tessa, if you'd like to prepare Theatre and scrub up, I'll operate and try to stabilise the stifle.'

Tessa nodded, briefly acknowledging Gus with a warm smile, the only moment she had had since being flung back into the busy Friday afternoon.

He grinned too. 'Lovely to have you back, Tessa. We've missed you.'

Sam watched them, his eyes cool. 'Hurry, Tessa, please. I'd like to get on as quickly as possible.'

She wasn't surprised at his abruptness. The atmosphere between them had chilled. Almost as though regretting his plea, he had withdrawn into himself during the journey back from Oxford. With tense nerves, she had arrived at the Hall just before lunch. Would Suzie be there? she'd wondered. Sam hadn't mentioned her, nor had he brought up the subject of the journalists again, but it was still a thorn in his side, she sensed. Dreading that one should appear, she had stepped out of the Porsche, only taking a deep sigh of relief when Greeley appeared, his calm face and disposition making her feel easier about her return.

Had she made the right choice? she had wondered as she'd washed and changed for work. Leaving her father to explain to Todd had been cowardly too.

She felt guilty about it. Todd had been a good friend for years. But the early start had left them no time for goodbyes and she had been relieved that Felix and Archie had stayed at friends' overnight, releasing her from the problem of explanations. Unexpectedly, her father had asked for none. Whatever discussion had gone on between the two men last night, the outcome had resolved in Sam's favour. With a niggling reluctance she had to admit that her father liked Sam, and he wasn't a man to be easily persuaded.

Work, in the afternoon, came like a balm on a sore. Sam had walked with her from Beechwood and they had both made reasonable attempts at conversation, but she'd known they would only be relaxed when they started a routine again. If Suzie had been at home, she hadn't shown herself, and it was only when Tessa began tying her surgical gown around her that she finally felt orientated once more, forgetting Suzie and the last miserable seven days, her scrambled brain actually reorganising under the discipline of work.

Sam smiled at her as they prepared in Theatre. 'Not too jaded?' he asked with a rueful grin. It was the first natural gesture he had made and she responded with a soft laugh, her green eyes sparkling.

'I think I'll make it.'

He pulled on his surgical gloves, watching her. 'Whose room did I sleep in last night?'

'The guest bedroom,' she answered, frowning at him, surprised. 'Why?'

He shrugged. 'The perfume on my pillow. It was yours.'

She realised her father must have borrowed a pillow from the airing cabinet in her room. 'You've got a good nose.' She laughed lightly, turning her attention away, fumbling with the steriliser clumsily.

'I wouldn't mistake it anywhere.' He came beside her and she sensed his presence although she didn't look around. 'As Gus says . . . it is good to have you back, Tessa. I've missed you.'

Knowing hot colour was rampantly spreading over her face and deeply shocked at the intimate admission, she struggled to regain her composure. When she finally looked up at him, her response came fractionally late.

'Honey's prepared,' he told her, distancing himself. 'I'll run over the brief outline of the op with you before we start.'

She had known many vets who adapted themselves to their work with dedication, but she had never felt an intensity like Sam's before. She sensed he had still not forgiven himself for losing Bruce. He was tensing, beginning to assimilate the work pattern ahead, getting his mind completely attuned. With a sudden understanding she knew she was part of the process of preparation. A pang of disappointment visited her. Was this the only reason he had wanted her back at Beechwood?

'I'm going to replace the ruptured ligament with a new one constructed from adjacent tissue.' She watched him make the first incision. 'There are a number of techniques. Have you seen a stifle rupture before?'

'Not exactly like this.' She paused, trying to think. 'I've helped with quite a number, but Honey's is rather severe, isn't it?'

He nodded, the grey eyes deep with concern. 'Retrievers are energetic dogs. She must have been severely handi-capped.'

She watched in admiration as he gently took the ligament from the tibia, passed it through the joint and over the lateral condyle of the femur. 'This is called the over-the-top technique — self-explanatory, really. Finally . . . ' he gave a customary sigh of satisfaction she was beginning to know off by heart when things went well ' . . . I anchor the section down, like this.'

It was incredible work. Tessa sighed too; the intensity of relief was enor-mous. 'And recovery? It's going to take quite a while, isn't it?' she asked, helping to clean the area.

'Mmm. Careful post-op nursing is imperative. You'll be able to play out all your motherly instincts with her.' He laughed lightly, giving her a swift, amused glance.

'She's going to be spoilt,' Tessa agreed with a smile. 'But after an op like this I think she deserves spoiling. I just hope her owners don't want her back too quickly.'

He shrugged. 'They will just have to be patient. Honey's joint will have to be protected while she recovers, probably two or three weeks of total rest. She'll be safer in a recovery pen here for a while.'

Tessa passed the suturing needle, hoping the McCormacks would be sensible about their pet's recovery and not demand her return too quickly.

Sam looked down at her. 'We'll work something out with them. Let's get her on to the drip, shall we?'

Tessa took it in turns with Sam throughout the rest of the afternoon to watch Honey. She was a strong, healthy dog and in spite of the complex operation she recovered well from the anaesthetic.

Shortly after five, an estate wagon pulled up in front of the surgery and a big red-headed man climbed out. 'Eustace Mayfield,' Sam said, peering out of the window. 'I haven't seen him for a couple of years. Runs a farm not far from here. Had a brilliant herd of milkers at one time.'

The man came in, followed by a sheepdog. After salutations, Eustace Mayfield shook his head and rubbed his chin. 'I don't like the look of Shep, Sam. Ears back all the time, no energy. He's getting slower and weaker by the minute. Like he's given up. Won't eat . . . and when he does he brings it back.'

'How old is he?' asked Sam as he examined Shep.

'Seven, going on eight. He's so tired he doesn't want to get up in the mornings. Like me, I suppose. Near retiring time. I should be sorry to lose him.'

'I hope you won't have to,' Sam answered with a reassuring smile.

'Can't go on like this. He'll disappear 'afore long.'

Sam nodded. 'I'm going to keep him in for tests, Eustace. I've got a feeling he might have a blocking disease, not too different from its human counterpart. Look . . . I don't want to say anything before I know . . . come in on Monday and pick him up.'

'I don't mind admitting I'm fair lost without him. I was just hoping he'd improve. Is there nothing you can do to buck him up . . . without me having to leave him here?'

Sam shook his head. 'Come on, Eustace, you know better than that.'

The farmer arched a thick, marmalade eyebrow at Sam and hesitated. Tessa could see Sam's profile hardening and she knew it was a contest of wills. But she had no doubt of the winner, though she did breathe a sigh of relief as the farmer nodded.

Eustace Mayfield shrugged. 'I know better than to argue with you.' He ruffled Shep's coat and left without protest.

'Poor old Eustace,' Gus expounded as he walked into the room, having overheard. 'He's really attached to his dog. It would break his heart if anything happened to him.'

'Nothing will.' Sam's glance caught Tessa's and she saw that same determination there, the sheer force of will-power.

'Got any idea what it might be?' Gus asked.

Sam gave a reluctant nod. 'Possibly myasthenia, but I won't know until I've done a few tests in the lab. In fact I think I'll take Shep in and begin right away.'

Tessa assisted Gus with the last few stragglers and was just sitting down in the office to complete the filing when Annie called from the adjoining door, 'Sam, you're wanted on the telephone — some sort of trouble up at the house, I fear.'

Sam hurried through and was back in a few moments, his face puzzled. 'Greeley seems to think he's caught an intruder . . . though what foxes me is what anyone thinks is of value in Beechwood. There's nothing you can take away in a hip pocket; you'd need a juggernaut!'

They all stared at him. 'Who is it, for heaven's sake?' Gus asked.

'I've no idea.' Sam looked at Tessa, frowning. 'Shall we go and see? Gus, we've more or less finished here, haven't we?'

Gus nodded. 'Take my twelve-bore if you like,' he joked.

'Firearms are no substitute for Greeley,' responded Sam with a dry laugh, smiling calmly at Tessa.

But her heart was nowhere near calm when they arrived at Beechwood and Sam shouldered the front door, not bothering to take his time.

'Good evening, sir,' Greeley said, his back to them as they rushed into the entrance hall. 'I'm sorry to have to disturb you at work.'

Tessa shrunk close to Sam as she saw Jay stiffen at their entrance, the dog's lips drawn back over his gums, revealing sharp white incisor teeth. Ready to spring, his hackles stood up like a wire brush along his coat.

'What's going on, Greeley?' Sam demanded.

Greeley stiffened, his face obscured from Tessa who stood quietly behind the two men trying to see who it was. 'Jay cornered him in the Great Hall, sir, and chased him to this point, where I intervened. Would you like me to ring the police?'

Sam shrugged. 'Nothing they can do that we can't. He seems to be frightened out of his life.'

'The seat of his trousers are, I'm afraid to say, a little the worse for wear. Jay has excellent reflexes. He is particularly alert at the moment while Juno is convalescing.'

The dog's snarling grew louder as a shaft of light caught the flaccid, frightened features of its quarry.

Tessa covered her mouth with her hand, trying to stop her gasp.

The face was unmistakable!

7

'Jay, down!' Sam commanded the dog. 'You'd better come out and tell us who you are — and what you want. The dog won't hurt you as long as you behave yourself. Or would you prefer to speak to the police?'

Tessa's lips parted on another gasp, the face of the driver of the car in which Suzie had been travelling burned into her memory. Quick to sense her reaction, Sam asked, 'Do you know him?'

She did not want to be the one to reveal Suzie's liaison; besides, she had no proof, just suspicion. Greeley said before Sam could ask her again, 'This gentleman has visited the Hall once before, sir.'

'Oh?' Sam paused, his brow dark. 'And who did you come to see?'

The man shrugged. 'I'm a reporter,'

he answered, squaring his shoulders.

Tessa felt momentary relief that she had not been wrong about Suzie, followed by immediate apprehension. In Sam's present mood, being a representative of the Press was the last qualification which would ensure his safety!

'And you think being a reporter entitles you to invade people's privacy?' Sam bit back predictably, his face angry.

'I came here for a purpose — a reason,' the man argued brazenly.

'Whatever your motives, you've trespassed, and trespassing is against the law.'

'You're Sam Wilde, aren't you?' the man persisted, ignoring the threat.

Sam frowned and Tessa could see his patience was running thin. 'What are you doing in my house?' Sam demanded again, his voice dangerously low.

'Call the dog off and I'll tell you.'

Sam brought Jay to heel. 'I'm waiting.'

'I came for the follow-up story, the one my paper has paid good money for. The story involving you and . . . her.' He glanced at Tessa.

She felt her body go stiff as Sam swung around, frowning at her, his eyes narrowed.

The idea of conniving with the reporter bred nightmares, but Sam's eyes fixed on her suspiciously. Was that what he was thinking — that the reporter had come to see her?

'Unless you want to give me your version of things?' the reporter pressed unwisely. 'A few lines, maybe?'

'This gentleman came here before, sir,' Greeley interrupted in a hard voice, 'to see Miss Granger, not Miss Dance.'

'You mean . . . Suzie?' Sam's face was a blank, not registering the implication. Suddenly, the truth seemed to dawn on him.

'Interesting . . . ' the reporter said, walking towards Sam. 'Do I take it there's been a little confusion in the family nest?'

'Nothing to the confusion I'll cause you,' Sam growled, 'when I talk to your editor and tell him I found you illegally on my premises!'

Tessa prayed the reporter wouldn't press his luck too far. Though Sam sounded in control, his hands gave away the inner disturbance as he clenched them into fists. 'You won't find anything here to interest you, except perhaps the colourful fantasies of Miss Granger's fertile imagination,' he told the reporter grimly. 'You shouldn't have coughed up the money, you know. Suzie's follow-up story would have been far more newsworthy if you'd tried making her wait for her thirty pieces of silver. Now you can get out of my home — and the next time you want copy, go through the proper channels and make an appointment. That way, you might get your facts straight.'

The man shrugged again and swaggered across the hall, flicking a card on the refectory table. 'Tell Miss Granger

I'm waiting to hear from her, will you?' Then he slowly pulled open the door and, with an insolent backward glance, walked out.

'Shall I serve tea now, sir, in the small drawing-room? Or would you prefer cocktails?' Greeley asked calmly.

The tension snapped suddenly and Tessa saw Sam's shoulders relax. He walked to the table, picked up the card, and tore it into pieces. 'I'll pour myself a Scotch. What about you, Tessa?'

'Tea would be fine.' She smiled uneasily.

In the small drawing-room, Tessa sat down on the old leather settee and watched Sam pour his drink, her legs just coming back to life.

He knew about Suzie now.

She was relieved for herself, but how did he feel about Suzie's deception? She wished it hadn't happened like this. The look on his face when he had been confronted with the truth had been almost too much to bear. He could accept that she, Tessa, had inadvertently given out foolish information, but coming face to face with a planned deceit like Suzie's was a bitter pill for him to swallow. She saw it just wasn't Suzie either. Women in general he held in low esteem, and Suzie's behaviour had done nothing to improve their image.

She gazed down into her lap and made a cat's cradle of her fingers, willing herself not to meet his face when he came to sit beside her.

She heard him tossing the ice in his drink and she wished Greeley would hurry up with the tea. Then Sam laid a cool brown hand on her arm, the electricity scorching her skin, forcing her to look up. 'It seems I owe you an apology,' he said, as he sat beside her.

'I'm sorry you had to find out like this.'

'Why didn't you tell me? You knew, didn't you?'

'Yes, I knew.'

'How?' He was staring at her, making her nervous.

'I saw Suzie with him, driving through the village.'

'And you didn't tell me?'

'How could I? Would you have listened? You would have thought it was sour grapes on my part. And I wasn't sure he was a reporter anyway. He might just have been a friend.'

Sam sighed, his brow creasing. 'Am I that unreasonable . . . unapproachable? Surely you owed me an attempt at an explanation?'

'I did try, Sam. I didn't want to accuse anyone else; I could have been wrong. I just hoped you would believe me in the end.'

He hesitated, a visible uncertainty in his face. 'You should have tried harder. Perhaps I was just waiting for you to convince me.'

She looked at him under her fair, thick lashes. 'Is that why you sent me away? Did you think I would cause more trouble for you?'

He shrugged. 'You could have. I thought you might still be upset with me for making that crazy pass. At first when the story broke I thought you'd either been naive enough to speak to a reporter who blew it all out of proportion, or you had deliberately lied ... it goes to people's heads sometimes, even a slight brush with the world of TV.'

'It didn't go to mine,' she said dully, feeling the backs of her eyes smarting. It was the worst thing in the world to be thought so badly of. And she hadn't deserved his suspicion. She stood up, trying to hide the hurt, walking with her head bowed to the mantelpiece. There was no blazing fire tonight. The hearth looked empty and desolate, the way she felt inside. But at least Sam had been honest with her; it took courage to be so honest. She sniffed, betraying the tiny pain under her ribs that she knew was deep, inner hurt.

When he gently turned her to face him, her eyes lifted to his, the green irises watery. 'Tessa, please don't be offended at what I've told you. Would you rather I had just kept quiet and offered you an empty apology?'

She shook her head, forcing back the wetness in her eyes.

'I . . . don't know how to handle you,' he confessed hesitantly. 'You're young — and truthful. It astonishes me. I'm used to dealing with people who put up façades. Even that reporter; I don't know him, I bore him no malice and yet look at his attitude. That's how a lot of people feel about you when you become successful. You don't know who your friends are, much less your enemies.' He pulled her gently to him, his face etched in a sadness that made her long to put her arms around him.

'I wish you knew me better, Sam,' she said, her breathing laboured. She tried to resist the temptation of raising her face to him but she yearned for the touch of his mouth to soothe away the hurt and an avalanche of memory lifted her stomach. She wasn't conscious of the right thing to do any more; all she was aware of was the need for him rising like a storm inside her. How could being happy possibly hurt so much? But this was happiness as she had never experienced it before, a feeling of complete and utter fulfilment in his arms.

'Look at me, Tessa.'

'Sam, I — '

'Being young and truthful doesn't give you any guarantee against me. The sexual chemistry between man and woman is most powerful . . . you must know that. And I'm beginning to fight a losing battle as I come to know you better.' He stared at her for a long moment, his eyes smouldering with an intensity which both scared her and enthralled her.

She didn't know what to do or say. It was heaven being in his arms, but he frightened her too. Was it his warning, or the torrent of rising passion within her own body that scared her so much?

Her skin leapt at his touch as he drew his fingers along the soft skin beneath her ear and down to her throat. His lips tasted sweet and hot when they found hers, drowning her thoughts and making her shudder as she eagerly responded, winding her arms around his neck, finding unparalleled pleasure in the feel of his hair. At first his kiss was gentle, probing, his fingers tightening on her back bringing in her small body to press against his chest. Then in hungry urgency his kiss became a demand and the demand a certainty that she could do nothing to stop him now.

Before she could divine his intention, warm fingers travelled over her buttons, his hands caressing the soft mounds of her breasts. Weak with desire, she allowed him to drift her into his tender lovemaking. In the drumming of her ears, she heard him breathing raggedly, pressing his lips into her hair. 'Tessa, you know where this is leading us, don't you?'

His words were softly persuasive, peeling away her resistance, and yet, as always, they held a warning. Could she stop now, if she wanted? Could she resist the driving temptation to fall headlong into an affair with him? Because she was on the very brink of loving him enough to forget the fact that Sam Wilde, the star, not the man, was making love to her.

'If this is a game, Sam,' she whispered uncertainly, 'then I don't know the rules.' Her green eyes looked up to him for understanding. 'I . . . I haven't played before.'

He stared back at her, frowning, taking in what she had just said.

She nodded, embarrassment creeping in scarlet waves over her skin. 'Does it make a difference?' she asked uncertainly, her voice barely audible.

He nodded slowly, the deep pleats in his brow becoming grave. 'Yes . . . yes, it does make a difference, a hell of a lot of difference. You certainly know how to cool a man's fire, don't you?'

'Sam . . . ' She was confused by his reaction. 'I'm telling you the truth; I have to. Your opinion of women seems — '

'My opinion of women, Tessa,' he interrupted her savagely, pushing her away from him, 'has nothing to do with you. I'm sorry — again. I shouldn't have done what I did.'

'But Sam,' she persisted, her heart aching already with his mood swing, 'it was beautiful . . . I mean . . . I wanted you to kiss me . . . '

'Do you know who you were kissing?' he asked incredulously.

She felt panic. 'Y-yes,' she stammered, 'I think I do.' Her fingers ran hectically over her buttons, fastening them. She felt chilled, as though the chasm was too deep for her to cross back to him. That whatever admission she had made had dampened his ardour and was reflected in the cold grey ice of his eyes.

He turned away. She watched his broad shoulders stiffen, as though inwardly he was taking stock of himself, easing himself out of the intimacy with her as though it were part of a well-practised routine. Her legs felt lifeless. She walked to the settee and sat down, only to jump as a knock sounded at the door.

'Come in, Greeley,' Sam said without even turning around.

Greeley walked in, seeming oblivious to the pall of tension that filled the room. He bore a silver tray set with china and lowered it to the coffee-table, shifting some magazines.

'Do you know where Suzie's disappeared to, Greeley?' Sam questioned him, making her look up in surprise.

'Yes, sir. Miss Granger has just returned home and has gone to her room.'

'Thank you. Tessa, don't wait for us at evening meal, Suzie and I will be eating out tonight,' he told her roughly, brushing past the settee without even giving her a glance. 'Greeley, tell Mrs Pearson, will you?'

Greeley stood silently as the door closed behind Sam. Tessa tried to cover her shock. She couldn't believe what had just happened. Greeley stooped and poured hot water into the teapot, a job which seemed to take forever as, in a state of helpless confusion, she forced back the tears which threatened to cascade.

★ ★ ★

Tessa opened the door to the kitchen and saw Mrs Pearson's stout, familiar frame labouring over the Saturday morning breakfast.

'Morning, dear.' Mrs Pearson grappled with a steaming dish of kedgeree and thrust it on to the range, pulling away the tea-towel quickly. 'Sit yourself down. There's fresh orange on the table.'

Tessa had had half a mind to skip breakfast, but she sat down and poured juice, not wanting to invite Mrs Pearson's suspicion.

'Help yourself,' Mrs Pearson instructed, bringing the dish to the table. It smelt delicious but Tessa had no appetite.

'Mrs Pearson . . . I really think I can only manage some cereal or fruit this morning . . . '

'Not you as well! What's happening to this household?'

Tessa looked up, her eyes puzzled.

'Mr Wilde and Miss Granger going off like that, never a word, all this food prepared and no one to eat it . . . '

'Mr Wilde's gone?'

'An hour ago. Didn't want a morsel, nor did she. Just coffee. Who's going to survive on coffee all day, I ask you?'

Mrs Pearson's speculation brooked no argument from Tessa; her heart wasn't in the subject. Sam had obviously meant to get as far away from her as possible, to sever whatever link had been tenuously forged last night. He didn't have to worry. She had taken the hint. It was big enough even for a naïve fool like her to see. He did not want to embark on an affair from which he might not escape unscathed. An involvement with an inexperienced female was just not palatable, despite the amusement she might provide temporarily.

Over the weekend, she had time to reflect on what she had done. Not only had she been stupid enough to think that Sam was interested in her, but she had abandoned sanity completely and confessed to the assumption, being promptly rejected when he had realised she had no experience within the framework of his sexual expectations.

If only she had stopped to think! Why in heaven's name would a man like Sam Wilde be even remotely interested in her? Her cheeks flared at the thought as she walked to the surgery on Monday morning, the painful memory of Sam's rebuff, compounded with his absence, making her think she must have been temporarily out of her mind to let him kiss her like that . . . to admit to wanting him to make love to her. It was a relief to see the Porsche was not parked outside. Wherever Sam had disappeared to with Suzie, he did not intend to rush back in a hurry!

Eustace Mayfield waved from his vehicle, parked it and ambled slowly to meet her. 'Frowning like that will give you wrinkles,' he laughed teasingly.

Tessa smiled self-consciously. 'Hello, Mr Mayfield.' He opened the door for her and surprisingly Gus stood there with Shep on a lead, wagging his tail.

'Shep!' Eustace's face lit up as he knelt and the dog padded into his arms. 'What's the verdict, Gus?'

Gus grinned. 'Sam's left you a course of drugs he is hoping will help Shep. Come into my room and we'll have a chat.'

The two men disappeared, leaving Tessa breathing space to get herself ready for the day. Whatever Sam's attitude to women, he never let a detail slip where animals were concerned. This knowledge twisted like a knife in her heart, weakening her resolve to harden herself against him. She admired him more than any other man she had ever known. Perhaps it was television which had deadened his real emotions to only needing to relate on a superficial level? Maybe nothing would eradicate the splinter of ice in his heart, which seemed preserved for posterity by women like Suzie.

★ ★ ★

The rain slithered down in sheets, caressing the small, neat windows of the surgery with noisy fingers. Monday was in with a vengeance and Tessa glanced at her watch, wondering if Sam would miss the afternoon surgery.

'We've half an hour until we open the doors,' Gus said, abstaining from voicing his own thoughts. 'I'll take the open clinic with you, Tessa, if Sam's not back.'

Tessa nodded, searching for something to keep her occupied meanwhile. She just couldn't concentrate. Sam never missed surgery.

She went into the recovery-room and took swabs and cotton wool to clean Honey's dewy eyes. She stroked her gently, ruffling the thick hair of her neck, and eased the soaked pads over her eyelids. She was coming along nicely, her stifle joint improving by the day, and she had reacted well to remaining still. Perhaps it was a lucky thing she was a slothful creature.

Absorbed in her ministrations, she barely heard the commotion outside. Male voices blended with the echo of the downpour on the veranda and she got to her feet, listening.

Was that Sam's voice?

She washed her hands, dried them, making herself go slowly. She closed the door to the recovery-room and walked into Reception, outwardly calm, pacing herself, feeling a little sick.

How should she react if it was Sam? Her eyes kept glancing at the clock and seconds ticked past, feeling like an eternity. When the door opened her heart stopped for a moment.

'Hi there!' A man came in, smiling at her. Behind him came another dressed almost indentically, they were shaking their heads like dogs after a bath. Both were clad in wet gear and wellingtons and had huge bags and tripods under their arms. Then came a small woman, her dark hair scraped back into a pleat, her fawn raincoat dripping wet.

'Tessa? I'm Marge Brinkley . . . series co-ordinator.'

'Boris Wakeman . . . sound man . . . pleased to meet you, Tessa.' She looked up into a young, fresh face of about twenty-five framed by a cloud of light brown hair.

'And I'm Damien . . . camera,' added the smaller, older man. 'Sorry about all this, dumping our stuff on you, but it's hell out there. Are you busy? Are we in the way?'

She managed to close her mouth and say that surgery hadn't begun yet.

'Sam told you we were arriving . . . didn't he?' asked Damien, lowering expensive-looking equipment on to a bench.

'You're the television crew?' Tessa murmured.

Damien grinned. 'Nothing for you to worry about. Just go on as usual. You'll find us crawling from the woodwork over the next few weeks, but you'll get used to it. Just treat us as part of the furniture.'

Then she heard more laughter. Her eyes strayed to the open door and she saw a tall, slender female figure. 'Hi, Tessa!' Nina Graham called.

Tessa raised the corners of her mouth hesitantly. She stared at Nina. High cheekbones and creamy skin made her even more attractive close up.

'I hope Sam hasn't been plying you with horror stories about filming?' Nina asked, drawing off her silk scarf.

Tessa hardly had time to reply. Her eyes shifted to the shadow walking in from the rain. She smiled, her heart leaping erratically. 'Hello, Sam,' she mouthed, the noise drowning her small whisper. In the general confusion she heard him shout to her and saw the trace of a smile cross his lips, but then more people poured in and she lost track.

Marge Brinkley and a busy little man with an armful of clipboards chatted to her. Tessa waited for Suzie's arrival, her heart continuing to thud heavily, wondering what reaction there would be when she came face to face with her. But as the door slammed she realised Sam had not arrived with Suzie . . . no one even mentioned her name.

'This place is just great,' Damien told her, shouting above the hubbub. 'And I can see why Sam wanted you in. Have you done any television work before?'

Tessa began to open her mouth to say she had barely discussed the filming with Sam, but something stopped her. These people were here at Sam's invitation. They weren't used to confined spaces, that was obvious, or the strict routine of a practice. But she just couldn't stop and gossip while people were lining up outside to have their animals treated. Irritation built up in her. It had been taken for granted that she would fall in with a sudden deluge of technicians. Gritting her teeth, she thought what her employer would say — Remember, Tessa — flexibility!

'No,' she replied, looking for Sam, 'I haven't worked in television. Er — would you excuse me? I think I ought to be getting ready for our clients.'

Fortunately Damien's attention was diverted and she managed to escape. Hadn't Sam remembered surgery was just about to begin? The little practice was bursting at the seams. Already the crew began to take stock of where they would begin filming, spreading a map of the Forest on to one of the tables. Amid the heads she scoured the room.

'Over here,' she heard Gus calling, and spotted his harassed face. With relief she saw Annie coaxing the crew through the adjoining door to their cottage in an attempt to make space. In their wake one or two clients made their entrance, dogs yapping and loud guffaws coming from Boris and Damien, who moved like acrobats among the equipment and the enquiring noses of dogs.

At last she saw Sam trying to clear the way. Clients filed in at a steady rate now, a clumsy blue Great Dane taking up most of the area in the waiting-room.

'We'll have the Dane in first, Tessa,' Sam shouted at her. And before she had time to think she was wrestling to lead the dog through into one of the treatment-rooms. Once landed, Frederick the Dane very firmly resisted Sam's attempts to give him his boosters.

'He was fine last time we saw him,' Sam complained, trying to coax Frederick from making himself at home under the treatment table. A fiercesome pair of black lips quivered and a white gleam of tooth prompted Sam to stand back.

'It's probably the disturbance outside,' Tessa said, wondering where Frederick's owner had got to. She peered through the door and saw the woman's head, bent in conversation with the man bearing clipboards. 'Our clients are more interested in what's going on out there than their pets.' She shrugged, looking back at Sam.

He grimaced and irritably called Frederick's owner. 'They would have to arrive on a Monday,' he muttered under his breath, his voice grim with frustration. 'I wasn't expecting them until mid-week.'

If you had been here earlier, she thought privately, you might have got things properly organised, despite when they were due to land!

With Frederick finally immunised and out of the way, Tessa hurried to find her next patient.

Sam frowned, staring at the cat she brought in. 'Who's this? Where is his owner? Don't say we've mislaid them again. What's going on?'

'Mrs Frobisher's Thomas,' Tessa introduced, her own temper beginning to fray. 'And Mrs Frobisher won't come in because she can't stand the sight of blood.'

'And I suppose we can,' Sam said with emphasis.

Tessa ignored him. 'Thomas has a bad ear and he won't let her have a look at it. She's sitting in Reception. Damien is keeping her occupied,' she ended with a wry glance.

'I wonder what makes Mrs Frobisher think we'll do any better than she has?'

Just as he bent to stroke Thomas, a burst of laughter penetrated the walls, voices carrying through from the next room in which more people had congregated. Sam whirled on his heel and thrust open the door shouting, 'Keep the noise down, will you? We're trying to work in here.'

Tessa wondered why he bothered. It was obvious the place was going to be turned into a TV set! She stroked Thomas gently, but the cat's instincts were already bristling to unleash themselves.

Sam returned his attention to her, his lips in a hard, straight line. 'I'm afraid we're going to have to put up with a little inconvenience for a while. I would have got them settled straight into Beechwood but Nina wanted to get the feel of the surgery.'

Tessa gathered the cat more firmly into her arms. She didn't need an explanation. She could see what was going on for herself. 'It's up to you, Sam, what you do with your practice.'

Sam frowned at her. 'Yes, it is. And we'll just have to work around them, that's all.'

She looked up at him, her green eyes cool. 'You don't have to remind me flexibility is all part of the job.'

'I won't need to remind you,' he barked, making the cat squirm in her arms. 'You've got it off parrot-fashion.'

'Your patient is receptive to your tone,' she reminded him airily.

'My tone . . . ?'

Tessa gently lowered Thomas on to the examination table, ignoring Sam's question. The furry body arched in disgust.

'Talk to him . . . or something!' Sam groaned in exasperation, bending into a yogic position to inspect the twitching black ear.

'What would you like me to say?' Tessa asked, trying to restrain a paw as Thomas lashed out, affronted at his treatment.

'Anything! I can't get near him. Hold him still!'

'Perhaps it's your bedside manner,' Tessa muttered as she leapt back, missing the claw. She immediately regretted having said it, but she was being provoked.

'And what exactly do you mean by my bedside manner? What's got into you?'

'Sam, I can't just wave a magic wand over him and make him docile. He even objects to Mrs Frobisher looking.'

'Cats have never worried you before. Do what you normally do!'

'It's not exactly a normal day, is it?' she bit back, watching the green-eyed ball of fur twist in Sam's arms as he wrestled to avoid the talons. 'You're just making him worse. He can sense you're impatient with him!'

'Impatient?' He glared at her.

'Yes, impatient. He knows it. He won't respond to being hurried.'

Sam's eyebrows shot up, his eyes glinting an angry silver. And, not as alert as his charge, he allowed Thomas to wriggle out of his arms and scoot around the door, which he had left ajar when yelling at the crew. 'Now look what's happened!' he complained bitterly, glowering at her.

'It's not my fault, Sam!'

'I didn't say it was.'

'I resent the way you're hinting at it.'

'And I resent being told I'm impatient. I'm never impatient. It's one of my rules.'

Tessa sighed, at the end of her patience. 'Well, you've broken it today, And I can see why.'

'You . . . what?'

'If you took more time in genuinely building up this practice rather than hosting a football team, you might find your temper wouldn't be so stretched over a fractious cat!'

The straight mouth fell open. 'You've got a nerve. Telling me my job — again!'

'I thought your job was with animals. I thought you were a vet!' she contradicted hotly.

He wagged a long finger at her, struggling for words. 'Ah ha! That's what's upset you, Miss Clever Clogs! For what it's worth, it's not the camera crew I have trouble with — or fractious cats — it's precocious young women like you who think they've got the answer to the meaning of life!'

She flinched, recognising some truth in the accusation, but who did he think he was, to tell her?

'You're the most selfish man I have ever met,' she choked out, her face flushed.

'You've made your opinions plain enough!' he shouted back, just as the door swung open and the lens of a camera whirred in on them.

'Smile!' shouted Damien, his face

puckered behind the camera, one eye creased up. 'That's fantastic!'

And Tessa discovered with a shock that the reflex smile on her face was as professionally forged as the one displayed by Sam.

8

Their smiles meant a precedent had been set.

It meant Sam had got his way and, whether Tessa liked it or not, she was involved with the filming. And it meant, so Damien was relieved to inform her, she was a natural for a camera angle.

Tessa was simply drifted into the stream of their work, finding her concentration shattered by the whirr of a camera, or an object rather like a hairy sponge drifting around in space above her head reminding her she was being constantly observed. If the Thomas incident was anything to go by — and Thomas was only a small cat — she wondered how Sam fared while filming the rather larger and more dangerous versions. Did he ask Nina to talk unruly lions into behaving themselves? Realising that her attitude was becoming almost as cynical as her employer's, Tessa avoided confrontations over the next few days, but one morning, when Sam answered the telephone, she found herself cornered in the same small space with him in the office. She wondered if his bad mood still prevailed. She took a step sideways, but he reached out, lifting a hand. When he put the receiver down, he quirked an inquisitive eyebrow at her. 'Where are you off to hide now?'

'In any corner I can find which doesn't conceal a camera lens or a mike,' she answered drily. 'But I don't think I've much hope of finding one.'

He chuckled. 'You really don't fancy a career in television, then?'

She laughed softly. 'I can think of easier things to do for a living.' The idea made her go cold inside after what she had witnessed this week.

'You mean, being propped in drastic positions all day? Saying half a dozen words twenty times and not getting it right? Being bitten around the ankles by midges and not letting it show?'

'Something like that.'

He shrugged, raising a sardonic eyebrow. 'The girls Nina hires get paid well enough. Then there's the prestige, the contacts for more television work for them. They don't object to a little discomfort. And you have to admit it comes out all right in the end. You've told me yourself you're a fan of the series.'

'Even more so now,' she agreed, smiling forgivingly at him. The filming had kept everyone on their toes. All things considered, Sam had kept his patience pretty well. 'But that doesn't mean to say I wouldn't feel the same about any subject with the right presentation,' she insisted; 'soap flakes . . . ice-cream . . . hair shampoo. If I've learnt one thing this week, it's that if the formula is right anything goes. Packaging is what counts, obviously.'

His grey eyes gently mocked her. 'So that's what you think . . . not very flattering, is it?'

She grinned. 'You get enough flattery.'

'But not from you?'

'Why should you want my flattery?'

'What male doesn't want a woman's pampering every now and then? Name me one.'

'Flattery and glamour wear thin after a while,' she parried, her green eyes very bright. 'Even television celebrities must get tired of it in the end.' She hesitated, looking up at him, her face instantly softening with regret. 'I'm not criticising. I know you're serious about your television work . . . it's just sometimes it doesn't seem very real.'

'But that's the way it has to be for a professional effect,' he defended quickly.

'Then I'm glad I don't have to face up to those sort of pressures. I don't think I could cope.'

He stared at her for a long moment. 'You cope with far greater pressures in surgery. I've watched you carefully. You've never panicked or lost control. You've always kept a level head no matter what's happened.'

'Two different worlds, as you've told me often enough,' she reminded him with a rueful grin.

'Do you think today will be free of fractious cats?'

She laughed with him then. It was good to laugh, to be at ease with one another. 'That wasn't the best day for either of us, I don't think!'

He put his head to one side, still laughing. 'Shall we escape today, make sure we aren't disturbed either by cats or cameras?'

She giggled. 'How?'

He eyed her with challenge. 'That was Eustace Mayfield. He said Shep is responding well to the Neostigmine I prescribed. I have the perfect excuse now to go out and check him. I need a good navigator, though . . . any offers?' As he dropped a kiss on her cheek, his fingers lightly touched her hair. 'I'm trying to make up for biting your head off the other day.'

She stared up at him, aware of the

fierce rhythm of her heart. 'What about the filming?'

'What about it? They will have to do without us. Gus can look after surgery.'

She grinned. 'I'd love it.'

Life with Sam was like being on a huge roller-coaster, emotions constantly see-sawing, as though she had no control over them. One minute she was telling herself she hated him, the next that she . . .

Tessa felt a flush run up under her skin. That she what? How did she feel about Sam Wilde . . . really feel? Confusion was something she had not had to deal with before. Sam had taken over her mind ever since she met him. Struggling against it was no use; she kept coming back for more.

'Let's get some things together,' Sam suggested, beginning to move about the office. 'Eustace said he'd like me to cast an eye over some Guernseys while we're out there. So I'll take that spare case of mine . . . if I can remember where I've left it.' He opened a cupboard, revealing an empty space. 'Stupid of me,' he grumbled; 'where have I put it?'

She stood still, waiting, as he rummaged into another cupboard.

'Now what did I do over the weekend?' He stood thinking, considering the floor. 'I called in to attend to a few things at my London practice . . . after dropping Suzie at the airport. No, I didn't take it in there, of course . . . must have been at Nina's flat. I took all my stuff in with me overnight because I didn't want to leave drugs in the car . . . '

Tessa watched him in shock, wondering how he could so casually mention that he had exchanged one woman for another! He twisted around, scratching his head, thoughtfully regarding her — and mistook astonishment for reticence.

'Not over-keen on farmwork?'

'No . . . I mean, yes . . . ' she mumbled, trying to control her befuddled brain. He always managed to lull her into a sense of drugged well-being just before launching some remark or action which devastated her. But what did she expect from a man like Sam?

'Then what are we waiting for? Come on, let's get cracking. Make the most of the opportunity while we can.'

Automatically she reached for the remaining case as he rushed off to tell Gus. Unmitigated gall was Sam's gift. And he used it liberally.

The soft rasp of the Porsche came from outside.

She had to give him credit. Sam Wilde was what Archie and Felix had summed him up as, though at the time they had been talking about his television techniques.

A very smooth operator!

★ ★ ★

Eustace Mayfield had a beautiful farm.

It spanned acres of grazing and crop land and his herd of British Friesians grazed peacefully under the hot sun as the Porsche prowled its way through Green Farm's gates and up the mud-caked track. 'Eustace has done pretty well for himself,' Sam explained, negotiating the lane with caution. 'I just hope he can persuade his family to go on with the farm when he retires. It would be a pity to see this little corner of England commercialised by a developer.'

'Oh, but it won't surely?' Tessa frowned as she peered across the lush pastures with its clusters of chestnut and oak, a verdant oasis in the heartland of the Forest. She was recovering from the ride on the roller-coaster, her heart just about settling back into place.

'Depends, I think, on whether or not it's still run as a family business. I know his older son; we were at university together. He's an academic, not a farmer. The younger son, Greg — I haven't seen him for years. Maybe Eustace has coaxed him into farming by now.'

'Did your father visit Green Farm ever?'

'Spasmodically, I'm afraid to say. He never had time to build up contact with farmers; he wasn't at home long enough. And Gus couldn't manage large animal work on his own; he had plenty on his hands with the village and the Forestry Commission.'

'So it was Shep who got you back together again?' Tessa asked, smiling.

'Or providence.'

Fleetingly he turned, their eyes met and she wondered what he meant by that remark. Despite her resolve, her guard melted to a warmth under his gaze. If she was going to react like this every time she looked at him, she had better remind herself of the way he treated Suzie and Nina. They had presumably fallen victim, too, to the same smile, the eye-contact, the intimacy with which he could suddenly make a woman feel absolutely the centre of his attention.

Sam drove the Porsche to a red-brick Georgian-style house — very neat for a farm, but she could see Eustace's personal stamp on it. Probably that was the reason why he had been such a successful farmer: his own way of doing things.

'Different, isn't it?' Sam swung open his door and climbed out.

'It's lovely!' She stood breathing in the farm air, a peaceful tranquillity about the place save for a distant mooing in the milking sheds.

'Hi, Sam!' a woman called, hurrying out to meet them from the house. Her greying hair, once very dark, Tessa imagined, was cut thickly to her neck in a youthful style and she had warm, welcoming eyes as she shook Tessa's hand.

'Betty ... this is Tessa,' Sam introduced simply.

'Eustace has told me a lot about you,' Betty Mayfield smiled. She glanced back at Sam. 'Will you come into the house for tea or do you want to begin straight away?'

Sam's eyebrows shot up. 'Begin what? I hope that husband of yours hasn't got anything too ambitious lined up for me. We were talking about Shep and a handful of calves on the phone.'

'You know Eustace,' Betty grinned. 'You'll find him with Greg and the farm manager in the office. You remember the way, don't you?' Betty took Tessa's arm. 'Meanwhile Tessa and I will introduce ourselves properly — over a cup of tea.'

Smiling ruefully, Sam walked away and Betty led Tessa into the house. It was completely modernised, with wide stairs, thick carpet and fashionable drapes at the windows.

'What a lovely house you have, Mrs Mayfield.'

'Betty, please!'

Tessa followed her into the kitchen, a streamlined breakfast bar spanning one wall.

'Yes, it is unusual, isn't it . . . for a farmhouse? Everyone thinks it's going to be old-world when they walk in. It was once, but Eustace and I redesigned it when Gregory came home.'

Tessa settled on a stool and watched Betty Mayfield make the tea in her bright kitchen. It seemed reflective of the Mayfields' characters, fresh and welcoming. 'Gregory is your youngest son, isn't he?' she asked, remembering Sam's description of the family.

'Yes — he's coming into the business. He's been at agricultural college and decided he wants to take over when Eustace retires.'

Betty brought the tea and set it down, producing some delicious cookies. 'Our eldest son works in London; he's a solicitor, hates the country. Greg's decision to come in on the farm has been quite a relief for us . . . so that's why . . . ' she gave a light laugh, looking at Tessa with frank eyes ' . . . we'd like Sam to take over the veterinary side. Eustace is going to try to persuade him today. He never managed it with Gerry . . . but now Sam's home . . . '

'Temporarily!' Tessa warned gently, knowing Betty Mayfield searched for a reaction to her comment. But what could she say? Sam was no one's fool. He would not like to be pressured in any sense of the word. 'Sam is . . . well, it's hardly for me to say, Betty. He is committed in other areas. Television . . . his practice in London . . . '

Betty sipped her drink thoughtfully. 'Yes. Television's a big draw, isn't it? I've warned Eustace not to be over-enthusiastic and thoroughly put him off the idea of coming back to large animal work.'

'You must know Sam very well,' Tessa commented, realising there was more to Betty Mayfield than met the eye.

'I used to see quite a bit of Else,' she answered, confirming Tessa's silent observation. 'She didn't really fit in at Beechwood from the very beginning. Then she met a wealthy businessman who offered her what Gerry couldn't and married him. I'm happy to say Sam and she made their peace before she died a few years ago.' Betty smiled, her voice unintrusive. 'Sam needs a settling influence. He's had no roots, no security on which to draw after Else went.'

Tessa nodded, reticent to indulge in gossip.

'Oh, Gerald was a marvellous father,' Betty went on heedlessly. 'But Sam was at boarding-school for most of his life, then at university, only coming home in the holidays and occasionally to help out at the surgery. In view of his background it's no wonder he's in between the devil and the deep blue sea.'

Tessa had time to ruminate on Betty's comments as she nibbled at the biscuits and listened to her lively chatter. She was rather surprised, though, when Betty stood up to remove the empty cups, murmuring with a deep frown, 'Sam seemed different today, Tessa — I can't quite say how. I haven't seen him in such a good mood for a long while.' She looked back from the sink, grinning. 'Wouldn't be anything to do with a woman's influence about the place, would it?'

Tessa watched Sam counting the number of respirations per minute on one of Eustace's new cows, her mind still on Betty's question. If Sam had changed at all, it would be difficult to put the transformation down to any one woman in particular . . . that was the joke! She'd refrained from saying so to Betty even in a light-hearted way. She didn't know her well enough. But she had left Betty's kitchen with laughter, deciding she would like Eustace and Betty Mayfield — if she ever had the chance to get to know them.

Eustace was sucking his bottom lip at the present moment, indicating the suspense as Sam prised up the cow's wet jowls.

'I was worried about that yellowish look.' Eustace pointed to the gum colour.

Sam, dressed in his overalls and wellingtons, shook his head. 'No, they're OK. You often get that with

Guernseys and Jerseys. It's quite normal.'

'That's a relief.'

Tessa had changed into her boots and overall and was thankful she had, for the afternoon's work wasn't the cleanest. With the slyness of an old fox Eustace had coaxed Sam into a full health-check for his cattle, sensing Sam's interest was stimulated from the start by the look of the barley-brown cows tinged with red, their bright eyes staring languidly out at the world.

The time had passed so quickly, the initial reason for their visit had been overlooked. Shep hadn't surfaced and Eustace's poor excuse for getting Sam to visit was conveniently forgotten. Sam was lost in his work, his eyes intent on the udder of the last cow he had examined. 'I'd like to examine the mammary glands and milk now, Eustace.'

'You're sure you've time?' the farmer asked, knowing he had no cause for concern now that his fish was on the hook.

Sam looked up, a wry grin on his face. 'You old rogue! Don't think I don't know what you're up to!'

'Me? Up to something? Never! I was just thinking . . . you don't cover many farms around here, do you?'

'No, I don't. And you know why,' Sam answered, smiling.

'Oh, yes, hmm.' Eustace shrugged, stroking a large chin. 'That sideline of yours . . . TV, isn't it? Must keep you pretty busy, I suppose.' He sighed again, watching Sam feel around the udder.

'What about my calves?' Eustace looked up and grinned connivingly at her, his broad, purplish hands spread out on his knees above his boots. 'You won't ever have seen ones like it. Prettiest things on God's earth. They need vaccinations, worming . . . '

Sam turned his face up and Eustace stopped mid-sentence, pushed out his lips and began to whistle.

'If there's time . . . if! Then we'll do the calves afterwards,' Sam retorted.

'Now let's finish off this little lot. No signs of diarrhoea, I take it?'

'None at all.'

Sam coaxed the lean, long-faced Guernsey to walk a few feet, watching her closely. Tessa picked up the soiled thermometers, depositing them in a bag for cleaning. She listened as Sam discussed the cattle. She was amazed at his tolerance of Eustace. The fact that they had known each other for such a long while must contribute to Sam's forbearance with the man, but, even so, since they had only really come to see Shep, Sam had been extremely easygoing in allowing himself to be drawn into the work.

Gregory came into the pens, a mini-version of his father, gingery hair and light blue eyes and a wide and friendly smile. He had helped during the afternoon, quietly taking it all in. Tessa frowned as she contemplated the one remark he had made to Sam which had worried her. 'I'm in your hands, Mr Wilde. I'm looking forward to learning a lot.'

Sam had flicked him an irritable warning look of which Gregory had seemed totally oblivious. She remembered an occasion before when she had inadvertently crowded Sam and suffered his abrupt reaction. In the young man's statement there lay a wealth of unintentional commitment. It was plain Eustace had brought Sam out to try to sway him into a positive response — to take Green Farm on as regular clients, even though he knew Sam was thinking of selling the practice.

'What about worming?' Eustace asked later as they came to the batch of calves. 'What do you suggest?'

Sam shrugged his shoulders and Tessa wondered if he was willing to be drawn. Unexpectedly he replied, 'I'd recommend vaccinating with Dictol. It's a little more expensive but absolutely worth it. These are particularly good calves.'

'I'm relieved to hear you say it.'

Tessa held her breath. Eustace smiled

and Gregory Mayfield glanced at her. It was an odd feeling, being among these country folk. She was even more alarmed when Gregory went on to ask, 'I've a friend in Rhillswood, Sam. He's got Ayrshires . . . bought the farm six months ago. He needs a similar sort of regime. Would you be able to find time to fit both farms in?'

Tessa felt clammy with anticipation, though she was unsure why. Perhaps it was because she had anticipated a negative response from Sam all after-noon and now he must surely give one!

'I'll be perfectly honest,' Sam said slowly. 'I'm not taking on farm work, simply because I can't guarantee continuity. And that's what you're asking me for, isn't it?'

'I'd be a fool not to, Sam. I need a good vet. I haven't had one I've really been able to rely on. It's a farmer's curse if he can't get himself a reliable vet,' Eustace admitted.

'I don't want to compound your difficulties,' Sam said with apologetic resolution. 'You won't thank me in six months' time if I decide to vanish.'

'I'll take the risk,' Eustace said stubbornly.

'And I'm up to my eyes in practice work at the moment . . . '

'I'll wait.'

'You make it very difficult for me to say no, Eustace.'

'That's because I want you to say yes.'

Tessa felt her legs go weak as she heard Eustace's grumbling laughter. She turned away, unable to look at Sam's face, gathered together the equipment which had been used and hurried to the washroom where she scoured it with frantic energy, the water chasing away the voices of the men.

It was a good half-hour later when, emerging from the washroom, all the equipment shiningly fresh, she saw Sam shaking hands with the Mayfields. It was the end of the day; she couldn't read any of their faces — all three of them looked tired and ready for some refreshment.

'Come into the house,' Eustace offered as Shep emerged from the barn. 'Have a meal with us. Look, even the dog's made an effort to come out and see you at last.'

They all laughed and Sam bent down to give Shep a quick examination.

'He's eating and keeping his food down. And as you can see he's deigning to put one foot in front of the other now,' Eustace said with a chuckle. 'Thanks, Sam, I owe you one.'

'You owe me nothing,' Sam returned tolerantly, 'until you get the bill.'

'I reckon I've got my money's worth.' Eustace gave a quick look towards his son.

'Be seeing you, then, Sam,' Gregory said, shaking hands and departing for the milking shed.

'I'm pleased you've got it worked out with Gregory,' Sam offered, his face serious. 'Now perhaps you'll be able to take life a little easier. Enjoy some time off with Betty.'

'Get under her feet, you mean?'

Eustace roared, horrified. 'No, thank you!' He nodded to the house as they walked through the balmy evening to the dairy gate. 'Are you coming in? Betty will be disappointed if you don't.'

'Betty will be nothing of the sort,' declared Sam. 'She's enough to do with the kids without producing extra meals. Send my best . . . we'll have to get back anyway. I've a feeling we'll have been missed.'

In the car, Tessa sat quietly, relaxing into the seat, leaving Eustace waving, his gingery grey head standing out like a beacon.

'Did you say . . . kids?' she asked, glancing at Sam.

'She organises groups for disabled youngsters. She's a very busy woman — and a very kind one.'

'Oh, goodness . . . and I was thinking how lovely it must be to swan around a house like that all day with nothing more to do than collecting roses in a basket!'

Sam turned briefly and gave her a

puzzled look. 'You really would like that kind of life?'

She threw back her head, laughing, undoing her knot of hair, allowing it to fall freely. 'No, I'd be bored within the hour,' she admitted. 'I need a lot of activity around me . . . Dad says I was hyperactive from a baby.'

'So what do you plan for yourself, if not a life of wanton idleness?'

She looked away, afraid of revealing too much. She didn't want to start talking in an intimate vein, and the question, though lightly put, was the kind which always led the conversation into deep waters. She shrugged. 'We couldn't have animals at home. Archie has an allergy to animal hair, so we had to miss out on a dog. I've promised myself I'm going to surround myself with animals one day, other than in the working sense. But I'd love to travel first, see something of countries I've only read about or seen on television — like Africa.'

'You haven't been abroad?'

'Just to Europe — school trips and once to Paris with a friend.'

'Would that be Todd?' he asked, casually.

A smile spread slowly across her face. 'No . . . it wasn't Todd. What made you ask?'

'Oh, just a guess.' His large hand encompassed the gear-lever and took the car down a notch. 'And after your travelling, what then?'

'Back to my house in the country, my animals.' She laughed flippantly.

'Alone . . . in your house? Surely you wouldn't want to be alone?' he prodded.

'I wouldn't be. I'd have my children!'

'Your children? Where do children come into your scheme? Have I missed something?'

She glanced at him, her heart beating fractionally faster. How had he managed to steer the conversation this far? She pressed her hands around her knees, hesitating. 'Two boys and two girls. I wouldn't mind in which order, though I'd like to have a son first. I think older brothers go better with younger sisters.'

'Isn't it rather risky planning out a family at this stage?'

'A calculated risk, maybe.'

The croon of the Porsche's engine uphill made her glance out of the corner of her eye at him. Calling his bluff had done the trick. He was looking quite pale.

'It seems to me . . . ' His lips moved pensively and she jerked her eyes back to the road in front. 'It seems you've got it all worked out. Would your friend Todd be figuring in any of these plans, by any chance?'

She took an inward breath, turning to gaze at him, 'Todd? No, I don't think so. Why ask me about Todd again?'

He shrugged, his profile silhouetted against the rush of hedgerow. 'Just a straightforward deduction.'

'Because I was out with him, that evening you came to collect me?'

'You both looked well suited. He's

your age, has the same sort of interests, I imagine. You've known him a long while.'

She nodded. 'We get along well, yes. He's always been around since Mum died. His parents helped out a lot afterwards, Mrs Greystone especially.'

Sam shrugged. 'In which case my deduction was right.'

She frowned, staring at the unbending features. 'No. It's wrong . . . if you're thinking there is more to our relationship than friendship.'

He turned his head briefly to one side. 'Suppose that were true . . . what happens if you hit a setback with this master plan of yours? Something incidental to the scheme — like not finding a suitable candidate to sire your offspring?'

She grinned, staring out of the window so he could not see the laughter in her face. 'Hmm,' she murmured, keeping her voice light, 'that would be a hitch, but only a technical one. I'd get over it somehow.'

The accelerator pedal went down. 'I believe you would,' Sam muttered, changing gear with dexterity, but with a look on his face which suggested the dexterity lay only in the way he handled his car and not in the manner he had handled the conversation with the young woman sitting next to him.

9

Honey was going home.

The McCormacks cheerfully listened to Sam, but Tessa could see they were nervous. Taking Honey back and getting her into a routine was going to be a new experience for the three of them.

Sam asked them to follow him into the garden and Tessa trailed behind with Honey, who ambled at a snail's pace.

Sam gestured for them to sit on the garden seat. Mrs McCormack clutched her handbag, sitting stiffly beside her husband, frowning at her pet.

'She's had several weeks of total rest,' Sam said in a reassuring voice, 'and she needs another before any lead exercise. Are you sure you want to take her home?'

'I miss her so much,' Mrs McCormack said quickly. 'And I don't work, so I can look after her all the time.'

'I'm for leaving her with you, Mr Wilde,' Mr McCormack said, glancing at his wife. 'Sick animals worry me. I think she's in the right place here. What do you think?'

Sam shrugged gently. 'There's an argument for both options. Honey's beginning to pine and that delays recovery. On the other hand, being in the confined space of the recovery pen, she's less likely to get excited than at home.'

'Honey rarely gets excited,' the woman put in. 'She's a phlegmatic dog, lazy, I suppose. I thought for the first week I'd keep her in the utility-room. There's not enough space for her to do any damage, it's light and warm and she has her basket in there . . . '

'A woman always has the last word,' Mr McCormack laughed easily. 'We'd better take her, Mr Wilde.'

Tessa handed the lead to Honey's mistress.

'Thank you so much, Tessa, for

looking after her. Look at the way she's looking at you. Was she any trouble?'

Tessa smiled, shaking her head. 'We didn't know she was there. She's been the perfect patient. If I ever have a dog, Mrs McCormack, I would like one just like Honey. She has a marvellous temperament.'

'She'd lick a burglar to death,' commented Mr McCormack wryly.

Sam laughed, getting to his feet. 'Have you brought your car to the side-entrance here? It won't be too far for her to walk.'

When the McCormacks and Honey had gone, Tessa began to clear Honey's pen. She removed her water bowl and the newspapers at one end and then the acrylic bedding which had prevented so successfully the development of pressure sores. Folding it up, ready for the washing machine, Tessa came across a green rubber frog that she had bought for Honey as a plaything. Sighing, she realised she had forgotten to give it to the McCormacks.

'You're going to miss her,' Sam observed, coming up behind her.

'Oh, just a little bit. She was such a lovely animal, so placid and affectionate. Grateful for every little bit of company.'

'Oh, dear,' Sam sighed, 'you know you shouldn't get involved with our patients — you're going to have withdrawal symptoms.'

Tessa grinned, but she had developed a little lump in her throat. 'I know it's stupid of me — '

'But love conquers all?' Sam supplied, his grey eyes teasing her.

'In this case, yes,' Tessa smiled, blushing furiously, suddenly aware she had not heard him use that word before. 'I'll get over it.'

'But will Honey?' Sam persisted in a dry tone. 'She'll have a restless night without her comforter.' He nodded to the green frog in her hands. 'It wasn't out of her sight, was it, while she was here?'

Tessa smiled and shook her head,

fingering the toy. 'They don't live far from the village; perhaps I could take it to them.'

'A good excuse to see Honey again!'

'No! Well, maybe yes. But I didn't deliberately keep it behind. It was tucked under her bedding.'

'I believe you — though thousands wouldn't! I'll run you there after surgery,' he said, grinning at her.

'I can walk,' Tessa protested, thinking it would be quite a relief to prolong returning to Beechwood. Crawling the way it was with people, the house had lost some of its attraction. Even Greeley was losing his cool.

Each night after dinner, they divided up into groups and she found herself making excuses to retire early or to phone home and make the call last hours. Or to go out for a walk, hoping Boris and Damien wouldn't suggest escorting her as they initially had. They were good company, full of fun and humour, but they weren't particularly interested in animals other than in a photographic sense and their conversation lay mainly in their friends back in London. And watching Sam and Nina together had begun to hurt if she stayed in the house. She had no right to feel hurt; she was nothing to him above and beyond an employee. He had known Nina for years. Why shouldn't he pay her attention, slinking his arm around her waist, laughing with her over cocktails, poring for hours over the filming routine? Sam never seemed to be without female company. There would always be a Suzie or a Nina in his life. Always.

'It's five or six miles to the McCormacks',' Sam said, her eyes flicking back to him. 'By car it won't take us ten minutes. As a matter of fact I want to call in and see Tom Hawkins and his dog. Do you remember, the one who had an accident with the trap?'

Tessa nodded. Was she likely to forget? She had met Tom on the weekend Sam had disappeared with Nina to London. It seemed an age ago now.

'I suppose if I asked what you were thinking I would no doubt get a truthful answer — which I might not like!' Sam sighed, his lips twisted in a puzzled smile. 'You've been miles away. And it's not Honey you're thinking about, so don't tell me it is! Your thinly veiled attention of late leads me to assume your job isn't the only thing on your mind.'

Colour rushed to her cheeks and she took refuge in walking to the laundry bin and dropping in the bedding. 'My mind is always on my work,' she lied. Well, it was not quite a lie, she told herself consolingly, just half a one. The other half was standing, staring at her with puzzled grey eyes.

'That's what I'm worried about. You don't go anywhere to enjoy yourself. Don't girls of your age like going out, enjoying a wild scene somewhere?'

She nodded, barely gazing up. 'I do enjoy going out; there just hasn't been very much time lately.'

'I would have thought your friend

Todd might have made time. He surely has been in contact with you?'

Tessa frowned at him. 'No, as a matter of fact I haven't spoken to him lately.'

'Not rung him — or written?'

His interest startled her. And why did he always bring Todd back into the conversation? She hadn't realised Todd had seemed to dominate her life so much that it was apparent to other people. But admittedly it was a little strange that Todd hadn't written or called her, running up someone's phone bill, probably the health farm's! Was he upset, she wondered suddenly, over her not saying goodbye the last time she was home?

'Archie and Felix pass on all the news,' she answered, reassuring herself as well as Sam, and then, seeing disbelief on his face, she asked drily, 'Trying to get rid of me again?'

'I've no journalists to be cross with now,' he smiled, 'only a rampant TV crew.'

As though the mention of the crew precipitated their appearance, a cry came from Reception. 'Nina ... I think,' Sam said, hurrying to the door.

'Sam!' A soft blur of moving colour came into Tessa's vision as the door opened fully. Nina was breathless as she rushed in, dressed in a cool beige top and figure-hugging leggings. 'Sam ... we've a few hours of light. Can I drag you away for a couple of hours into the Forest? Our scout has located deer, about twenty of them.'

'What type, do you know?' Sam asked, frowning.

'Haven't an earthly. We're townies, remember? That's why we need you, darling.'

Nina frowned apologetically, and laid her hand on Sam's arm. 'Do you mind if I borrow him, Tessa?'

'Of course not,' Tessa quickly replied, trying not to look disturbed. 'Gus and I shall be here until this evening.'

'Have you mentioned next week to Tessa, Sam?' Nina asked, and Tessa jerked around again, her eyes wide.

Sam shook his head. 'No. I'll leave it to you to do the honours. I'll go and change into some casual clothes in the office and be with you in a couple of minutes.'

Nina watched him go then peered into the empty recovery cages. 'We shall have to get a few shots in here,' she said idly and Tessa had the sinking feeling she always got when bad news was close at hand. Nina said, 'We're planning a surprise party for next weekend. Sam thinks it will be best to have it at Beechwood Hall and we want you to be there, Tessa. So keep the Saturday evening free.'

Tessa knew she had no excuse, that she was trapped. She said hesitantly, 'What — er — kind of surprise is it?'

Nina's smile radiated secret pleasure. 'It would be giving the surprise away if I told, wouldn't it? But I'll give you a clue. It has something to do with this.' She streched out a slim finger, decorated by a solitary ring, a circle of tiny rubies mounted in gold. They sparkled as Nina twisted her hand. 'No one has noticed yet. It just shows you what an observant lot men are!'

Tessa stared at the ring, her eyes widening, her body going cold. 'It's very beautiful,' she managed, her voice thick. No wonder Sam had left the room quickly! After all his bravado — he was no different from Archie or Felix or Todd when it came down to women. Sooner or later, for all their talk, men had to abandon their independence to a woman . . . the right woman. Or was it the most persistent woman? Looking up at Nina, she managed to smile. 'I'm very happy for you both,' Tessa said, quietly. 'Congratulations.'

'Don't forget,' Nina said, her eyes shining. 'Mum's the word.'

★ ★ ★

It was almost seven by the time Tessa set out for the McCormacks'. She had changed into white cotton trousers and a pale blue T-shirt at the surgery, wrapping her cardigan into her shoulder-bag beside the green frog. There was even more reason now not to go back to Beechwood tonight.

The late June evening was fragrant and she sniffed in as she walked through the village, past the green and the shops and the Crossed Keys. Summer visitors were sitting on pine benches, drinking and eating. The sun was a scarlet saucer going down behind the trees and the road to the McCormacks', as Gus had directed her, lay eastwards out of the village, dotted with New Forest ponies and their foals browsing on the grass. Some lay bathing in the sun, others cast an interested eye towards the pub, where the smell of food trickled from the kitchens. Tessa walked briskly ahead, slapping away the midges as she passed through little clouds of them.

Why hadn't she guessed there was something more serious going on between Nina and Sam? She felt a fool. It was so evident now. Suzie must have posed a real problem for Sam. That was why he'd dumped her at the airport and then hurried to pour oil on troubled waters with Nina.

His kiss had been something to pass the time with. A distraction. Oh, why had she allowed herself to be so stupid? And why now should she be so concerned about his feelings for someone else?

'You're heading the wrong way!'

She almost jumped out of her skin. The Porsche had crept alongside her, the passenger door hanging open.

'This is the road Gus told me to take!' she insisted, recovering her composure, bending down to look in.

Sam put his foot on the accelerator and revved. 'The road has just forked . . . didn't you notice? Now stop arguing and jump in!'

She paused fractionally, but there was no excuse to refuse. 'You shouldn't have bothered coming,' she told him, sitting in and slamming the door. 'I would have found my way.'

'And probably been wandering out here at midnight, the rate you were going. Look . . . this road leads off on to the heathland; the fork you should have followed bears right.'

She sat quietly, her heart thumping as he reversed and fed the car into the right fork. All she wanted was to be alone for a while, get her bearings, and she hadn't been too bothered whether she found the McCormacks' or not. Just walking would have settled her down; it always did. Now she was in a confined space with the one person she wanted to avoid tonight.

'Why didn't you wait for me?' he asked after a while.

'You were out, chasing deer.'

'But I had told you I would drive you to the McCormacks' tonight. I wouldn't go back on my word.'

She had to force herself not to stare at him, amazed. Not go back on his word? That was a joke!

'Did you find your deer?' she asked, keeping her eyes on the road.

'Yes . . . and no.'

Her curiosity got the better of her. She looked at him out of the corner of her eye. 'What does that mean?'

'It means they found the deer, but they were just fallow, nothing particularly unusual. And I decided . . . not to take them to where the others are.'

'Others?' she questioned, not understanding.

He nodded, as the car came to a halt and the noise of the engine died. He leaned his arms across the steering-wheel and turned his head, staring at her. 'The Sika deer. They are the most beautiful creatures . . . very rare, just in scattered handfuls in certain areas of the Forest. I thought that was what Nina was talking about when she said they'd found deer.'

'What are so special about Sika?' Tessa asked soberly.

He smiled. 'They take a lot of beating; just a glimpse of them

— which is rare — and you feel you've witnessed magic. And today I just didn't like the thought of watering down that magic, strange as it might seem.'

She frowned at him. 'But isn't the filming about revealing the secrets of the Forest to people, to make them appreciate its beauty?'

Sam sat back, shrugged. 'Hmm. That's what I thought at first . . . are you ready?' he asked, changing the subject swiftly. 'Here we are. Honey's home.'

Confused, Tessa forced her eyes out of the window to the McCormacks', a rambling, Tudor-style house, with shaven lawns and an ornamental fountain. Sam had climbed out while she was still thinking over what he had said. She didn't understand him. Why change his mind about filming the Sika deer?

Jean McCormack greeted them with a relieved smile. 'Oh, Mr Wilde . . . Tessa, I was just going to telephone you. Bill says I'm fussing over nothing, but I'm worried about Honey. She's so different; she isn't eating . . . '

'May I take a look at her?' Sam asked.

'Please, do come!' Eagerly Mrs McCormack showed them through the house and into the kitchen. 'She's in here, the old utility-room.'

Honey lay comfortably in her basket, but her eyes drooped and she barely wagged her tail, lying quite still as Sam approached. Tessa laid the case down which she had brought from the car and Sam took out his stethoscope and began to examine her. Then he checked her wound, very carefully making sure she had done no damage to the stifle repair.

'There's no need to worry, Mrs McCormack, she's fine. I suspect the day has just been a bit tiring for her. You'll have to be patient.'

'But she hasn't eaten a scrap. And that's so out of character for Honey.'

Tessa searched in her bag and

brought out the green frog. 'Mrs McCormack, may I give her this? I forgot to give it to you this morning.'

'Of course, dear. How kind of you.'

Tessa knelt beside Honey and presented the frog. Honey sniffed at it, then gave it a lick, nudging it with her paw and making it squeak. Her ears went up and there was a distinct wag of her tail.

'Tessa — I think you've done the trick . . . look at her expression!' Mrs McCormack laughed.

And it was true. There was a pleat of fur on the dog's forehead giving her that alert, doggie look and her nose suddenly glistened with moisture. 'Wouldn't it be wonderful if she was just missing that?' her owner gasped.

'She associates it with being pampered,' Sam said wryly. 'Tessa gave it to her shortly after she regained consciousness. It was a daily routine — the two of them playing with it. Dogs have fantastic memories and associations.'

'Sam means I spoiled her thoroughly and I shouldn't have,' Tessa whispered softly as Honey licked her fingers and picked the frog up between gentle teeth for Tessa to squeeze.

Mrs McCormack touched her shoulder. 'I can't thank you enough . . . both of you. Honey means so much to us.'

Finally, after several attempts at trying to leave, but with Mrs McCormack intent on making them stay for tea, Tessa and Sam said goodbye to Honey, who had miraculously recovered her appetite and was tucking into her supper.

'You weren't the only one having withdrawal symptoms,' Sam smiled as they climbed into the car. 'It's a good thing we came out this evening.'

Tessa sighed. 'I won't make the mistake of getting too involved with an animal again. I felt terrible tonight, very responsible. I can't think what possessed me with Honey. You know, I've never done it before.'

'She came along at a crisis in your

life. You gave her all your affection. Honey had a crisis too . . . it was a question of timing. You both got it exactly right.'

'Do you really think that?' she asked, amazed, staring at him.

'Of course I do. Timing is very important.'

'But what crisis — of mine — are you referring to?' she asked self-consciously, her colour flaring up.

He smiled and shrugged. 'Maybe the change in lifestyle? You have to admit it has been quite a radical one for you.'

The Porsche crept up a steep hill with embankments on either side and into a lane. She hadn't realised they had been going deeper into the Forest. Sam's comment disturbed her. It hadn't been the change in lifestyle, though. Her crisis had been an emotional one and it had gone far deeper than changing jobs and homes!

'Where are we?' she asked, looking ahead, intent to get off the subject. A small cottage with a green fence lay on one side of the gravel lane. Dogs barked from the garden and geese and chickens strutted across the path, fluttering in front of the wheels.

'Tom Hawkins' place.'

Tessa peered out. 'It looks a bit overgrown.'

Sam laughed. 'He's eighty-four, one of the oldest commoners in these parts! How he manages what he does I'll never know. And be prepared for dogs . . . he's any amount of them!'

Almost immediately, three or four dogs came running from the house, spaniels and crossbreeds, barking noisily. They barked solidly at their heels as they walked through the gate and up the garden path.

Tom Hawkins laughed in the doorway. 'They'll simmer down in a moment! Come on in.'

Inside, the cottage smelt of dried fowl and dog food, sacks of which leaned against the walls. He made them sit down and quite suddenly half a dozen chickens flapped in, one flying up on to the back of Tessa's chair. Then the dogs charged in and there was bedlam and Tom took his shotgun down off the wall and shook it. To Tessa's surprise, the birds paraded out through the front door.

'They know I won't use it, except on human rumps!' Tom said with a cheeky grin. 'But there's no harm in threatening.'

Sam laughed at Tessa's shocked face as he settled down to examine the spaniel at his feet. 'Tom doesn't shoot — just gives a poacher or two a nasty scare sometimes.'

'I had a bird once,' Tom explained, 'a pigeon. He was half dead when a dog of mine brought it in in her mouth. Had a pellet in its side . . . do you remember, Sam?'

'I remember,' Sam said, his head bent down to the dog.

'Sam took the pellet out . . . he was no more than seventeen. Home on holidays, weren't you, lad?'

Sam looked up and smiled. 'That's right, Tom.'

'He was upset — and I couldn't fathom out why. I used to fancy a few plump pheasants in those days, or grouse. Killing things with a gun was humane to me then. Till Sam made me promise to keep this darned bird . . . which I did — to my eternal regret.'

'He died?' Tessa asked, glancing down at Sam.

'No! The damn thing lived for years. Spent all its life getting fat on old Tom, followed me everywhere I went, even to the village. Sat on the dogs' backs, created a din every time someone knocked at the door, just took over the place. Do you think I could shoot ever again? Nope. I sort of viewed birds differently somehow. And practically everything else drawing breath. Can you imagine, a bird changing a man's life?'

Tessa kept her eyes on Sam, her gaze flickering over the strong back, the gentle fingers turning back the hair on the dog's paw. He had an incredible rapport with animals; with, as Tom said, anything that took breath. She could understand him better as she grew to see him through the villagers' eyes. The trouble was, the more she heard from them, the more she felt she knew the man beneath, a totally different character from the Sam Wilde presenting the right image to the camera.

'He's as right as rain,' Sam was saying cheerfully. 'No limp as far as you've noticed?'

Tom shook his head. 'Gus did a good job on him, Sam.'

'How about your other bitch? The one I came to examine a few weeks back? How did she do with her whelping?'

The old man grinned. 'Grand. A litter of three. No trouble at all.' Tom looked at Tessa and smiled. 'Would you like to see them?'

She nodded, her eyes searching the room. 'I didn't realise you had puppies here!'

'Follow me. They're in the kitchen by the Aga.'

She heard their playful whining, tiny yaps and miniature growls. Tom pointed to a corner and she gave a gasp. Three beautiful plump yellow puppies peered from a box. Beside them in her basket lay the mother, a thick-coated golden dog. 'Oh . . . ' Tessa glanced at Tom imploringly. 'Will she let me close?'

'Buttercup's as daft as a brush. Help yourself.'

Tessa knelt and stroked Buttercup first. Her eyes were exactly the same as Honey's, round and deep brown with tiny dark lashes. Buttercup looked as though she had some Labrador retriever in her, for she was stocky and broad-faced with a curly coat and a wet black nose. She licked Tessa's hand and rolled over in her basket to display her very fine feeding equipment. Out toppled the puppies from the box and soon Tessa was swamped. They smelt of milk and their little tummies were so fat they looked out of shape. With all three in her lap, Tessa had difficulty in retrieving her hair, a new object of interest for them to nibble at.

'We would stay if we had time,' Sam said, raising his eyebrows at her.

She cupped the little bottoms in her hand and placed them one by one back in their cosy box. They soon settled, one of them persistently awake, regarding her until she fell out of sheer tiredness on to her sister.

'I'm going to have to drag her away,' Sam said, and Tom laughed.

'They need good homes, Sam, so if you hear of anything . . .'

'I'll let you know,' Sam said, grabbing Tessa by the arm.

The two men talked on their way out about the illegal traps. She listened vaguely, the puppy smell in her nostrils, the feel of their hot, wriggling bodies still on her fingertips. This was a lovely cottage, untidy and dishevelled, but warm with love. Tom radiated a well-being and so did his animals. At least the little pups had begun their lives in an atmosphere of peace and harmony.

Tom offered them home-made wine but they refused, Sam having to drive and Tessa feeling a glass of wine would at this moment probably have a debilitating effect on her. She had to keep a firm watch on herself. She enjoyed being with Sam so much. She gave a little inner sigh, knowing the evening was almost over. This was a different world out here. The peace of the Forest did something to a person, like an invisible suit of armour. She just hoped some of it would rub off on her!

Soon they left the cottage, with the old man waving them off from his front porch beneath a shawl of honeysuckle, the dogs haring madly along the lane beside the Porsche then turning back for home.

'He's great, isn't he, for mid-eighties?' Sam said, adjusting his driving mirror. Then he looked at her. 'You're quiet.'

'Am I? Probably just ready for a hot shower and an early night . . . ' She hesitated. Should she congratulate him on his engagement to Nina? He knew Nina had told her. Was he waiting for her to say something? Somehow the words got stuck in her throat.

'Did you like the puppies?'

She nodded, sighing. 'They were beautiful! Buttercup reminded me of Honey.'

Sam chuckled. 'You've got that dog on the brain! Look, it's not dark yet. If you could hold on a while longer for that shower, I'd like to show you something.'

She frowned, turning abruptly. 'It's quite late, Sam, and it has been a long day.' It was like eating a delicious cake, being with Sam: the more you ate, the more probable the chance of indigestion!

'This won't take long. You won't regret it.'

She shrugged. 'Oh . . . I suppose so. Can't you tell me what it is?'

'A surprise,' he said with a grin.

He tried to take her hand.

'I can manage . . . '

'No, you can't. This is rough territory. With those flimsy things on your feet you'll be lucky if you get a few yards. Now hold on tight to me.'

'I didn't know I was coming . . . here!' She tripped and clung on to his hand and he grinned at her.

'No one knows about this place. You'll have to be very quiet.'

The silence was deafening. The green glory of the Forest was almost too much to take in at once. They had been walking, it seemed, for hours, but it couldn't have been very long. There was just a little daylight left, the silhouettes of the trees growing darker. Suddenly Sam put his arms around her and pulled her down. 'Shh, be very quiet. Whisper only.'

It was almost impossible even to do that, for the pounding of her heart was so extraordinarily fast that she had no breath left.

'Through there,' he whispered, sliding an arm around her body, tucking her into him so they could both peer through the fern, the dry grass supporting their body weight. 'Sikas. Two of them. Make the most of this, Tessa, for it's a rare sight.'

'Oh,' she breathed, trying to ignore the sensation of his closeness radiating electricity through her, 'they *are* beautiful!'

'Sika stags. The males are rich golden-brown on their backs, with that black stripe running along their spines. So distinctive. Just look at those antlers — aren't they phenomenal?'

Tessa caught her breath at the magnificent animal. She had never seen deer so closely before, much less the Sika stag.

'Notice his white rump . . . you'll see it as he turns to graze. Don't move an inch or he'll see you.'

She couldn't move. She was spellbound. The creatures, so gentle-looking, grazed by moss-bound banks under dark, ghostly green trees, illuminated faintly by rays of light. Sam closed his arm more tightly around her as they lay. As the darkness settled, she tried to pick out details of the animals she could remember. Their proud necks, the distinct colouring with that zebra stripe, the way they moved, so agile, with all the weight of the antler on their heads. It was difficult to concentrate. She was disturbed by Sam. Snuggled into him, her heart was really pounding.

'Listen,' he told her, his whisper dying in the silence, 'very carefully.'

There were no adequate words to describe what she heard. One of the stags raised his head and made a high-pitched whistle like a scream plummeting down to a groan. It was the most evocative sound she'd ever heard in all her life, making tears come into her eyes. Too quickly, the pair melted into the undergrowth and she was left with a feeling of having witnessed the magic he had told her about.

'That's the last we shall see of them,' Sam said regretfully.

She moved a little in his arms. 'I can hardly believe what I've just seen,' she breathed. 'I understand what you mean by magic.'

She looked into his eyes, her mouth open slightly, and she knew he was going to try to kiss her. It wasn't fair. This was such a special moment — and she so desperately wanted to share it with him. But she couldn't!

She shifted, moving out of his reach.

'Why are you moving away? Let's savour this little piece of heaven, Tessa.'

'How can you say that?' she croaked hoarsely, her chest heaving.

He eyed her curiously. 'I brought you here because I wanted to share it with you. I've never brought anyone else. It's a place I used to come as a boy.'

Why was he telling her this? He should be telling Nina, not her!

'I thought . . . this would be a good place to talk, without interruption.' He frowned. 'What are you thinking? I can see accusation in those green eyes. But why, I wonder?'

She rolled on to her side. 'I think we'd better go now. Thank you for bringing me to see the deer . . . '

'Stop being so polite and talk to me. Does it cost you so much that you can't sit still for once?' He reached out for her arm.

She outmanoeuvred his fingers and stood up shakily, looking down at him. 'I want to go.'

'And I want to talk to you.' He looked up, his forehead creased in dark lines.

'To talk to me? Is that all you've got on your mind, Sam? Or is it something more devious?'

His lips compressed tightly. 'I suppose you've every right to say that, but I assure you, tonight I just wanted to talk to you — away from prying eyes.'

She made a sound in her throat, a half-gasp. 'Nina's eyes?'

He whitened. 'You're not making sense, Tessa.'

'Aren't I?' She was trembling, going clammily cold. 'Let me make myself plain, Sam. I should have said this earlier, but now is probably the right time anyway. And you needn't have hurried out of the room when Nina told me; I wouldn't have given you away if you thought I'd speak out of turn . . . '

'What the blazes are you driving at?'

'What?' she repeated incredulously. 'Your engagement, of course! To Nina.'

He sat up, one arm casually resting over his knee, the other long leg stretched out. 'Ah . . . I get your point.'

'You do? Oh, I'm so pleased!' She was resorting to juvenile sarcasm but she had taken enough. The smug grin on his face was unbelievable!

With an easy, effortless movement he reached up, snatched her wrist and brought her into his arms, his mouth hot and wild on hers as she fell back into the grass.

She heard him whisper, 'Nina and I aren't married yet. There's still time for a little fun, my sweet Tessa.'

10

She kicked wildly.

Sam had hold of her wrists and he was strong. He pinned her on her back in the grass and bent to kiss her again, his hard body coming down on her. His mouth was persuasive, intent on arousing a response, and Tessa began to melt unwillingly under him; he was breathing life again into her need for him. It was true, Nina and he were not married yet. Would they ever be married? the voice of temptation asked inside her. She wanted him so much, she yearned for his lovemaking with a desperate hunger. It was a passionate, dangerous emotion, heedless of people's feelings, as it was now of Nina's.

Skilfully his hands left her wrists and curled around her body and she moaned softly, letting out a languorous breath, hating him for his deceit and herself too. Why was she allowing him to do this? It was wrong.

She was vaguely aware of his hand slipping under her waist and levering her up towards him. The image of his hand possessing Nina's waist came back into her mind. 'Stop it . . . stop it, Sam!'

'Why?' he whispered in her ear. 'I want you.'

She pushed against him. 'You want me — now! When you know something is forbidden, you want it. Not when you can have someone fairly,' she ground out, the memory of his rejection of her still an open wound. 'Loving is like a game to you — no, not loving, you don't understand the meaning of that word. It's challenge and conquering.'

'Don't think about words! I told you, they get in the way,' he persuaded temptingly.

'How can you do this? How can you go behind Nina's back?' She swallowed, fighting her want of him.

'You want me, as much as I want you.'

'Not this way.' She pushed herself, rolling into the grass, desperate for breath. 'I don't have any interest in being the first woman to jeopardise a marriage that hasn't even begun yet!'

Somehow she managed to stumble up, seeing his face as she went, the cynical twist of his mouth. He laughed aloud, staring up at her. 'Quite a little moralist. Is this how you've managed to keep up there in that tower of yours? Constantly keeping your men in a state of adulation — at arm's length?'

'Were you born cynical, Sam?' Her lips trembled. He could be so hurtful.

'No.' He shook his head, leaning back on his elbows. 'Cynicism comes with practice — lots of it.'

'Then I'm sorry for you,' she said, pity in her voice. 'Because you must have wasted a lot of time.' She began to hurry to the car, afraid for a moment that she might have let him go too far, for there had been a response from her body to him and he would know that. Her brief but active compliance under his kisses had given her secret away. But how could you keep love a secret? In spite of herself and in spite of him she was in love. It should be a time of joy. He had denigrated it, making her feel a pawn in his game, and she wasn't! She would be no one's plaything.

The car was parked a fair distance away. By the time she got to it Tessa was out of breath and a few tears had escaped down her hot cheeks. Her hair had fallen from the ponytail and was scattered about her shoulders like tossed corn. She fell against the warm metal, closing her eyes. She mustn't let him see her like this. She had to regain her composure somehow. OK, she loved him, she'd made the worst choice in the world, but then did you have any choice when your heart took over instead of your mind?

There was a stream she had noticed when they arrived and so she went to it, kneeling down on the mossy bank, dipping her fingers into the water. The coldness felt wonderful on her face. Her white trousers were grubby at the knees and grass ears stuck into her T-shirt. She pulled them out, reminding herself of the daisy-game. He loves me, he loves me not, he loves me . . .

Would Sam Wilde love anyone, ever, but himself?

She quickly splashed more water on her face, letting the drops soak in. That was better. She could face herself and her emotions again; they hadn't run away with her. She was still in control.

'Cooling down?'

Turning around, he was standing there, hands in pockets. 'You can't blame a man for trying,' he said, without a shred of remorse in his voice.

'I don't blame you,' she answered, standing up, her cheeks stinging. 'But just keep your distance from me, Sam. I told you I'm not interested in your games and I mean it.'

He shrugged. 'If that's the way you feel,' he agreed, casually, 'I'll behave.

But you will have to help me. You will have to stop looking so beautiful,' he drawled with charm in his voice, grinning as though he wouldn't hurt a fly. 'I'll be serious,' he added, feigning a contrite face. 'I'll even shake on it, if you will.'

She clenched her hands into fists. She didn't trust him an inch.

'Oh, come on. It was just a man's last try, think of it like that. Give me your hand and we'll shake on it. Your silence — and I'll leave you alone.'

So that was it! He had decided he had better try to keep her quiet. Well, he didn't have to worry. Silence was golden as far as she was concerned. Uneasily she held out her hand.

He held it, firmly, his fingers wrapping around it, then with a charming grace he pulled it to his lips and kissed it, making an army of prickles go down her spine.

She dragged it away quickly as his eyes teased her. 'Shall we get going?'

The journey back was the biggest

surprise of the day. After the way he had behaved, he acted as though butter wouldn't melt in his mouth and talked all the way home. She sat, her fingers clasped together, her heart pounding again.

When they reached Beechwood Hall, he swung the car into the drive and with a conspiratorial wink which made her want to hit him he put a brown finger to his lips and, as Nina swept down the steps to meet them, whispered, 'Shh, now. Don't forget, not a word about our being in the Forest together. We have a bargain, don't forget.'

* * *

On Wednesday, she heard from Mrs Pearson that some of the crew and Nina were going to London to see Leo Sheldon, the producer. Mrs Pearson draped herself over the table, shaking her head. 'I'll be glad when they're gone for good. I hate to say it, but these yuppies don't appreciate the meaning of good food. Look at it!'

Tessa stared at the silver dishes. Bacon, eggs, kippers and mushrooms, all left from breakfast. 'Breaks my heart, it does,' the older woman complained bitterly, turning some of it into Juno and Jay's bowls. 'I hate waste.'

'They aren't used to home cooking like yours, Mrs Pearson,' Tessa supplied, eyeing the leftovers, thinking there was no way someone like Nina or the half-dozen models who had arrived would entertain the idea of all those calories. Tessa sighed, thinking of Nina. She mostly thought of Nina these days and Sam and the looming prospect of her immediate future.

Sam had kept his promise. But there was something in his mood she couldn't understand . . . he was simply too nice! Was that because he felt such a snake in the grass? He deserved to be concerned. He was a Philistine! Suzie had been dispensed with because she was too dangerous to have around.

What was Sam thinking in that dark head of his about her? Sometimes she would catch his glance as they were working and he would grin. She had to turn away; she couldn't bear the message of those eyes. They both knew she had been a hair's breadth from letting him make love to her. It was almost like a threat: he would try again.

The morning was quiet and Gus and Annie decided on an early coffee-break. 'No clients, no cameras, no cuts!' Gus laughed, dunking a digestive into his drink. Just as Tessa sat to enjoy hers, Sam walked into the office.

Annie called, 'Coffee, Sam?'

Smiling, Sam's gaze caught Tessa's. 'Please, Annie.' Then, turning to Gus, he said, 'I've decided to take Green Farm on. What do you think of the idea, Gus?'

With surprise on his face Gus said hesitantly, 'First class . . . terrific! But what made you change your mind? I thought taking on farm work was out of the question?'

Sam pulled out a chair and drank the coffee Annie handed him. 'Let's say a slight change of plan. I'm — er — I'm thinking of expansion . . . '

'Really?' Gus gasped, amazed.

'Wonderful!' said Annie, a little lost for words.

'You mean . . . you're going to keep the practice on? Not sell it?'

Sam shrugged ambiguously. 'I'm going to ask Paul Lancing, my locum in London, if he would like to come in on a partnership. He knows the ropes pretty well at the London end and he's looking for something permanent. That will leave me free for down here. How do you feel about the practice, Gus? Would you consider helping me out?'

Tessa watched the older man's facial expression range from utter astonishment to delight. He glanced at his wife and Annie came over and slid her arms around his neck, kissing the shiny brown skin of her husband's forehead. 'Do you have to ask him, Sam? Don't you know?'

Sam laughed. 'I have to admit I was counting on a positive reaction.' He stood up, placing his mug firmly back on the desk-top, his grey eyes dancing. 'Good! So what better time than to start now? Tessa, pack my cases, would you? We'll be doing vaccinations at Green Farm, probably over a couple of days. Get together some of your old clothes — while it's quiet here we might as well get cracking. Gus, can you and Annie hold the fort?'

'I think we can manage that, can't we, Annie?' Gus answered wryly. 'Have you any more surprises in store for us, Sam?'

'One or two.' Sam grinned and turned to Tessa. He threw her a look of pure innocence. 'But I'm saving those for later.'

Tessa looked away. She was not going to give him the gratification of crumbling under those grey eyes, or of acknowledging a conspiracy — whatever it was. Sam had a method to everything he did, she had discovered that. She was as shocked as Gus and Annie at the about-turn. No doubt the answer would be evident soon.

But not until the second day of the vaccinations, when Eustace Mayfield was herding his cattle into a pen and Sam was absorbed with the measurement of drugs before he began a new batch, did she begin to get an inkling of what was in his mind.

It was late on Friday and Tessa was beginning to feel the first thread of stiffness tighten her back. She had been bending over to the calves and now she ached for a soak in a long hot bath.

Eustace Mayfield laughed, his glance catching the hidden stretch she made. He drew her aside, steering her out of the cowshed into the fresh air. 'Our difficulties all seem to have been resolved . . . I've been wondering, what made Sam change his mind?' he asked her, glancing back over his shoulder, though Sam was well out of earshot.

'About accepting your work, Mr Mayfield?' Tessa frowned. She knew the farmer was as surprised too. But even if she knew, she would not be at liberty to discuss Sam's business. As it happened, he had not confided his reasons to her, not even in Gus, who was the obvious choice.

'Not just Green Farm's work, but Gregory's friend too. And the rumour is going around fast, Sam is in Beechwood to stay,' the farmer told her eagerly.

'I . . . I honestly don't know, Mr Mayfield,' she mumbled. 'Sam hasn't talked to me about his reasons for expanding the practice.'

'Or quitting the television?'

Eustace Mayfield's question suddenly rang every conceivable bell in her head. Why hadn't she thought of it before? Now the pattern of events began to clarify in her mind. Sam had new horizons as a married man! He was going to concentrate on his veterinary work — and why? So that Nina could continue without impediment from him in the television sphere. It was the sort of sensible, successful reasoning that was to be expected from a man like Sam and an independent career woman like Nina. They had decided to go their own separate ways professionally in order to give their relationship a chance — as veterans of the TV world, they would know the risks involved. Some sacrifice had to be made and it looked as if Sam had backed down. Nina must be a very strong personality. She would be exactly right for Sam. She had probably brought pressure to bear after the Suzie episode and, with an inner sigh, Tessa realised it was only the toughest of women who would ever handle a man like Sam Wilde.

Avoiding the farmer's rhetorical question and making small talk, she managed to change topic. It was the end of the week and there were only a few more cows to be vaccinated. Her brain ached from continually thinking. And now she had worked out what was going on, she felt listless and empty. Jealousy still nudged its painful way under her ribs.

When she and Sam drove home from Green Farm, the late June sun hid behind a herringbone sky, tails of white cloud blown irritably across a blue sea, and her emotions felt in a similar state, leaving her flat.

'Looks like rain,' said Sam, with a smile that for some while now had really irritated. Did he have to be so happy? Could he dismiss the way he'd kissed her — and her response — so easily to the back of his mind? How could a person be planning marriage one minute and trying a hand at seduction the next — with different people?

'You may not get a good night's sleep tonight . . . it's only fair to warn you . . . '

She turned, half listening. 'Sorry . . . what did you say?'

He grinned. 'The ballroom . . . Greeley and an army of women have been working on it all day and probably will all night. It hasn't been used for decades. But Nina and I decided to let the moths out for tomorrow.'

She had forgotten. Had it come so soon, the party?

'Cheer up. It's not a wake. It's an engagement party. An excuse for a good time,' he told her unnecessarily.

She hesitated, concentrating on the white line in the middle of the road. 'Actually . . . I may not be able to come.'

'Rubbish. Of course you will.'

'I haven't anything to wear!' A pitiful excuse it might be, but it was the truth. She had practically nothing suitable. There were three or four summer frocks but nothing she could wear to an engagement party.

'Take tomorrow off and buy something! Why don't you take Annie with you? She'll make good company.'

'What about Gus? He won't cope with surgery on his own.'

'I'll be there. I need a good excuse to get away from Beechwood. Nina will be driving back down from London

tomorrow with the team and with Leo
— it will be chaos.'

With her excuses shattered, Tessa sat
grimly, contemplating Saturday. There
was only one way to get through it and
that was to smile! It wasn't every day
she was given *carte blanche* to go off
and spoil herself. She might as well try
to enjoy it!

The trip the following day was so
totally unexpected that she and Annie
laughed almost all the way. They took
turns at the driving and Tessa enjoyed
the stimulation of being behind the
wheel again, even though the Land
Rover was like a truck to drive. She had
learnt to drive in Archie's old Citroën,
painted every colour under the sun and
with a clutch as hard as iron. The Land
Rover had its good points. It was dark
green and inconspicuous and people
didn't turn to stare, and there wasn't an
enormous grinding every time you
missed a gear!

In the seaside town of Stourspear
they sipped coffee from tall glasses,

frothed with cream, before eating strawberries — a decadent but delicious breakfast. She hadn't been on a shopping spree since before leaving Oxford and being with Annie, who coaxed her into trying on almost every pretty dress they saw, was fun. They raided the stores in the high street, guzzled shellfish on a breeze-blown quay at lunchtime, and found the perfect boutique, hidden in a cobbled street, designer labels dripping off every item. The gown Tessa chose was a frosty green, the colour of her eyes, calf-length, body-hugging and silk, with a Chinese collar and no sleeves.

Annie chose a flowery two-piece, kind to her curves, which she admitted were in all the wrong places.

'Do you think we've spent enough,' Annie asked with a rueful smile as they visited the last shoe shop, 'or should we try that little jeweller's over there and break the bank hopelessly?'

There was no indecision between them. Tessa bought glittering oriental studs for her ears and Annie settled for a charm bracelet. They drove home on a high and Tessa had forgotten that she had been shopping in celebration of Sam's engagement. As Annie dropped her back at Beechwood, Nina's white coupé was the first car she saw, parked next to the red body of the Porsche. After that, there were too many cars to count.

Annie shouted goodbye as Tessa fumbled her parcels into her arms and slid out of the Land Rover, just managing to slam the door with her toe.

'See you later!' Tessa called, listening to the laughter coming from the house. Her heart sank. There would be dozens of people she didn't know, conversations to make, trying to look as if she knew who so-and-so was. 'Don't be late!' she called as second thoughts to Annie.

★ ★ ★

Beechwood's ballroom had been closed and shuttered since Else's time. Tessa had never seen behind its closed doors. Tonight, they were open wide, and every chandelier burned brightly, reflecting diamonds on the old, ornate ceiling. A quartet played on a raised dais, a deep gleam enhanced the highly polished wood floor and heavy red drapes lifted back from the long open windows, allowing the summer night to creep in like an uninvited guest.

'Do you fancy a dance with a man who boasts two left feet and a shuffle?' Gus held out his elbow gingerly. 'Hang on to it and I could lead you straight into disaster!'

Tessa laughed softly, clutching his arm, thankful for a familiar face. 'Where's Annie?' she asked, peering over his shoulder through the dancers as he twirled her erratically on to the floor.

'Dancing with the producer fellow.'

'Leo, you mean? He's nice, isn't he? I like him.' Tessa recalled the quiet bespectacled man whom Damien had pushed forward to greet her. For a producer, Leo disappointed her. He was not at all flamboyant as she had imagined, but rather an introvert. His smile was warm, though, and his handshake firm.

Gus growled as he almost trod on her toe. 'Sorry. Out of practice.'

Tessa clung on, still breathless at the elegance of the room. 'This place is wonderful, Gus. I can imagine what it was like in the old days.'

'Many moons ago,' sighed Gus. 'Things certainly have changed . . . and one of them is my waistline. I don't remember ever having so much trouble fitting into a penguin suit!'

He gave a little hop and a jump to the music to impress her and Tessa laughed.

'Don't laugh too much,' he warned her, 'they'll think you're crying with pain.'

After dancing with Gus, Damien and Boris monopolised her and then a string of other men who she supposed were all to do with the television unit. Her feet ached madly.

Greeley suddenly appeared from out of the crowd. 'Miss Tessa, there is a telephone call for you. A Mr Greystone, I believe.'

'Todd?' She was suddenly apprehensive. She hadn't spoken to him since that night . . .

Greeley left her in the library. She picked up the phone, her heart hammering. 'Todd?'

'Tessa?' His voice was faint. It wasn't a good line; there was a lot of static in the background. 'Have I caught you at the wrong time? You sound out of breath.'

'No! It's wonderful to hear you, Todd. Did dad explain everything to you when I left?'

Todd told her amid a crescendo of crackling that Joe Dance had explained. But she was beginning to have a strange feeling in the pit of her stomach. Todd's voice was different, almost apologetic. She found herself waiting apprehensively as they talked.

'Tessa, I've tried to tell you this

. . . remember the girl I introduced you to at the party — Amber?'

'The girl with brown eyes?' she asked. 'The pretty one?'

A little pause came. 'Yes . . . listen, Tessa, she and I . . . we're getting married.'

She almost dropped the phone. Todd was getting married?

'We're having a sort of celebration tonight . . . I felt guilty about not writing or phoning to let you know . . . you do understand, don't you, Tessa?'

She swallowed. 'Yes . . . yes . . . of course I do.'

'You're happy for us?'

Her mouth was dry. 'Very happy. It's wonderful news, Todd.'

She realised how difficult it must be for him, but at least she understood the silence from home lately. It was difficult growing up with someone. You loved him or her but in a totally different way . . . she had known the painful, passionate experience of her love for

Sam. For Todd she would always feel a sisterly love. But it was still a shock to hear it like this. The line was fading. 'Be happy, Todd!' she shouted and the line went dead.

The room seemed very still.

A moth encircled a tasselled lamp-shade until it found the bulb beneath. Then, discovering the warmth, it flew blindly around inside, the shadow of its tiny wings casting gigantic reflections across the bookshelves.

She felt like the moth. Small and insignificant against the power of light, except in her case it was the power of love. She wasn't quite sure what she should do. Her legs had the most peculiar sensation running the length of them. She shouldn't mind at all about Todd getting married, and if she'd been less preoccupied with her own problems at the time she probably would have guessed it last time she was home. Amber was a very pretty girl and Todd had virtually thrust her into their company. At any other time, she would have picked up the hint straight away.

'Bad news?' Sam stood in the doorway. How long had he been there?

'No, not really. No . . . not at all.'

'Like to talk it over?'

She fought back the tremblings of her lips. 'It was just Todd, a surprise . . . he rang to say he's getting married. To a very nice girl. Her name is Amber.'

How she found her face buried into his chest she didn't know. But Sam's strong arms were around her and he was stroking her hair as she fought to control herself, standing stiffly in his arms.

'And was it a shock?' he asked gently, his voice rumbling under her ear.

'Mmm. I suppose so. We've grown up together. He was my best friend when Mum died . . . living next door, always there. He was like a brother; one who listened and didn't tease. I'm happy for him, tremendously happy . . . '

Gently he lifted her chin and in the dull light of the room she was aware that his features had softened. She dragged her eyes away and made herself breathe again. She shouldn't be reacting like this. It was just one shock upon another that had finally brought the tears close.

'You don't look it. You look pretty miserable to me. Do you think it's wise to give him up without a fight?'

She gazed at him, her eyes very wide and bright. 'You still don't understand, do you? I don't feel like that about him!'

'But this is a pretty big reaction for a girl who says she's not in love with someone,' he objected with logic.

'It isn't a reaction to Todd!' Tessa protested, tracing a finger under her eyelid. This was ridiculous. She was behaving like a child and Sam was making it worse.

She moved away, sighing. 'I went to a party with Todd when I was at home. He introduced me to Amber and I thought what a pleasant girl she was. I just feel so stupid that I didn't understand.'

'That will teach you to go to strange

parties,' Sam muttered with a wry smile. 'You should have stayed at home and waited for me.'

'I did wait for you, all week!' Tessa wailed, the confession out before she had time to think.

He moved closer. 'Did you? That wasn't what you said before. You told me I shouldn't have expected you to hang around waiting.'

She turned her back to him. 'You're confusing things . . . '

'Am I?' He gave an insulted chuckle. 'That's not quite true. If anyone is confused, it's you.'

She gave a sharp gasp and turned, her green eyes flashing. 'What exactly do you mean by that?'

He eyed her drily. 'What I say. You seem to have Todd worked out all wrongly and you've known him for most of your life. What can be said for a poor soul like me, who's only known you a matter of months? What's going on in that little mind of yours, I wonder, about me?'

She turned her head away biting her lip. 'I don't have to think about you, Sam, not any more!'

'Oh, don't you?'

Seeing him standing there in the dinner-suit, his dark charm coming over in waves, however could she bring herself to lie like this? He had a world to conquer, ambition and drive, and a beautiful new wife who would be exactly the right person for him. That was what she thought of Sam Wilde on the surface. She would never admit to what she thought privately, to the terrible ache that remained with her day and night when she thought of the impossibility of her position both in an employed sense and a personal sense. What would happen when he was married? How easy would it be to live on at Beechwood and would Nina even allow it, even if Tessa could cope with the situation? She couldn't stay on and keep sane, surely?

She closed her eyes and then angrily

opened them again. 'Your guests will be wondering where you are!'

'Come here,' he said, grinning.

'No, Sam.' She stiffened, aware that he was walking towards her.

'Look me in the eye,' he commanded her as his fingers reached out and brushed her bare skin, bringing her arms out in a shower of goose-bumps. 'Tell me you didn't enjoy the way I kissed you, the way . . . we . . . kissed. Tell me.'

She ought to leave right now, get out of the room while she could, but he had a strange power over her.

'No denial?' he laughed mockingly. Then with tender eyes he said, 'You're beautiful, Tessa,' and his eyes flickered over the green dress, the soft ivory of her throat, the rise of her breasts as she tried to contain herself. 'But you're a very misguided young lady. You think you're right so often. I have to admit that was probably the way you managed to boss your brothers around — and it worked. But it won't work with me. I

311

warned you once and now I'm going to prove to you: you haven't a chance in a million of escaping me.'

She shook her head, feeling totally numbed. His brows knitted together and he stared at her lips, which began to quiver. Her whole body seemed raw as he held her in his arms, his breath on her cheek. Oblivious to the outside world, Tessa did not hear the door open.

'Tessa . . . where have you . . . ? Oh, Sam!' Nina's narrowed eyes fell on them. 'So this is where you've both been hiding!'

Tessa blinked, her green eyes as round as moons. 'No, Nina! It's not what you think . . . '

'It is exactly what she thinks,' Sam said in an amused voice, folding his arms around her waist. 'Don't try to deny it, Tessa. We've been caught . . . and we'll just have to own up.'

Tessa couldn't believe her ears.

She stared at Nina, her jaw dropping, trying to disengage herself from Sam.

'But it's not true, Nina!' she bleated, and knew by the look in Nina's eyes that she had no hope at all of being believed.

11

'Don't let them tease you, Tessa,' Leo Sheldon grinned, kissing Nina's cheek. 'The sooner you find out how to handle their cranky little jokes the better. The whole crew's a pack of mad hyenas. Haven't you discovered that yet?'

'She's learning fast,' Sam observed, watching Tessa's astonished face.

'You've missed the champagne toast!' Nina frowned at them. 'Come and help us to celebrate.'

'They're busy,' Leo told her, drawing his fiancée to him, kissing her again. 'Leave them alone. They're enjoying themselves.'

Nina giggled. 'I can see that. But aren't you both going to wish Leo and me luck?' She arched her neck to lean back into Leo's arms and murmured. 'We shall need rather a lot of it, I think, working together . . . and living together — legitimately!'

'I give it a week,' Sam chuckled and to Tessa's surprise Leo and Nina burst into laughter. 'OK, maybe two,' he added generously. Going to Nina and kissing her lightly on the cheek, Sam murmured, 'Congratulations to you both . . . you're a lucky man, Leo.'

He threw a glance back over his shoulder. 'Tessa?'

She jumped at the crisp clip of his voice. 'Oh . . . yes, congratulations . . . I'm very happy for you both.'

'I've been overworking her,' Sam apologised, his lips in an amused twist as he walked back to Tessa, swept her into the curve of his arm and, grinning, added, 'but I mean to correct that little mistake.'

'See you later,' Leo laughed, steering Nina towards the hall.

'We'll catch you up.' Sam smiled and turned his eyes back to Tessa as the library door closed.

He propelled her around in his arms, his fingers linking powerfully together at her back. He gave a low whistle as she stiffened, her face pale. 'I can see by the look on your face that I'm not in your good books. It was only a joke, you know.'

'I can't believe you would let me think . . . ' Tessa began, her voice dying under his amused scrutiny. She twisted resentfully in the circle of his arms, feeling the hard pressure of his thighs against her.

She stared at him dumbly. The laughter was gone from his voice now, but his eyes were still teasing. It was incredible! He had been dangling her on a piece of string . . .

'You'd better say something. You're beginning to worry me.'

'I . . . ' She shook her head. 'I don't know what to say!'

'That is unusual.' He gripped her tighter. 'You could get mad . . . and shout!'

'Why embarrass me like that, Sam?' she demanded, her hands pushing at the firm muscles of his upper arms.

He shrugged. 'I've been playing you

at your own game, young lady. You accused me of games, but I rather think it was the pot calling the kettle black.'

'You let me think you and Nina were engaged!' she exclaimed resentfully.

'You wanted to think it. I just didn't contradict you.'

'But you told me you stayed with her in London!' she spluttered, the accusation out before she could stop herself.

'I did, didn't I?' He laughed, his eyes sparkling with mischief. 'I forgot to mention it was Leo's flat as well.'

'You deliberately misled me?'

'No . . . you misinterpreted me.'

'How could you, Sam?' she bleated, wriggling, trying to set herself free so that she could be convincingly angry.

He laughed with renewed candour and ran a firm hand to cup her shoulderblades, steadying her. 'Oh, extremely easily. How could I let the opportunity pass? Your little mind was working overtime, drawing all the wrong conclusions. I could hardly let you down.'

She gazed at him, her breath coming quickly, her skin flushing, her brain whirring. She had to have time to think.

'Please . . . let me go . . . '

He shrugged, releasing her. 'Just as I was beginning to enjoy myself.' He leaned against the wall, hands deep in his pockets, an eyebrow arched as he watched her. 'I think we've some talking to do . . . but it can wait. I've waited this long; I suppose a few hours more won't make any difference. I patiently watched you dance with every man in this room tonight.'

Had he watched her? She had searched the ballroom constantly for his tall figure but only caught glimpses of him. She felt as though she was in the middle of a landslide, escaping with a few cuts and bruises, her legs trembling and her pulse banging like jungle tom-toms. She was forced to reassess him now, in the few minutes since Nina dropped that bombshell. The ripples were still washing over her, her mind recalling the times she had added her own impetuous nuance to his word or action.

He laughed, watching her steadily from across the room. 'Oh, I'm sorry, Tessa . . . just look at you, frantically trying to puzzle it all out.'

She glared at him, her cheeks on fire.

Suddenly he was beside her, taking her in his arms possessively and this time she did not resist. 'Forgive me?' he asked, his voice growing husky.

She looked helplessly up at him. 'There's nothing to forgive. You're right . . . it was my own fault.'

He ran a finger across the curve of her eyebrow. 'I want to kiss you . . . very much. May I?'

There was warm invitation in his eyes.

She lifted her face and his fingers journeyed through her hair, massaging her scalp. Shivering, her body arched involuntarily. His mouth descended, at first gently inquisitive, then fiercely with growing hunger. 'Oh, Tessa, what a fool I've been. How I've struggled not to love you.'

She gasped, stunned and disorientated, unable to move as his hands came up to catch her face and he repeated himself, forming each word slowly, looking into her eyes until she felt she would drown in those grey pools. Was he really saying he loved her? What did the words mean to him? How many times had he said them before?

'Sam . . . ' She muttered his name, her lips silenced by his kiss, deep and penetrating. Her hands lifted unbidden to explore his body, the broad curve of his shoulders, the hard muscle of his arms as he kissed her with a desperation that made her giddy with joy and reciprocal need.

Between tight teeth he groaned, 'All this time we've wasted. I've wasted. I wanted you so much, do you know that? Couldn't you guess?'

'But I told you . . . ' she stumbled, the question of her virginity having led her into deep and troubled waters before.

He shook his head fiercely. 'You

shocked me,' he muttered, his brows jerked together. 'Imagine, a man who covets his bachelorhood, determined not to make the mistake of trusting a woman . . . and then — you! I didn't have a say in it. I was shaken rigid. I had no defence against you. You told me you trusted me, so I tried to frighten you off. It didn't work. You told me you had never played my kind of game before . . . I just couldn't handle it for the moment. You devastated me.'

She shook her head. 'I didn't mean to.'

'It was because you didn't that I fell in love with you. Every woman I've ever known has always schemed or planned to make an impression on my life. You didn't. You kept confronting me with pieces of logic or truth. You were the most infuriating woman I had ever met.'

'Do I still infuriate you?' she asked, her voice low.

He grinned at her. 'All the time. Which is why I'm kissing you and telling you I love you. You can see how much you upset me.'

'Sam . . . '

He laid his fingertips gently over her mouth. 'Do you want me, Tessa? As I am? A very fallible human being?'

'I want you,' she gasped as he took his hand away. 'I don't want to change you or make you fit into a category. I just wanted to see more of the person I have grown to . . . ' She felt the words stick in her throat. The most precious words of all; she had longed to say them to him and now she was dumb.

'Say it, Tessa!'

She looked at him with surrender in her eyes. Her voice was soft, barely audible. 'To love you . . . to love you with all my heart.'

She meant utterly, all her heart. But though no person was between them, no superficial demand threatened her outright love for him, a recollection lay in the shadows.

Suzie's ghost hovered. Or maybe it was the ghost of all the women who had shared his life. She was having to face the revelation that he loved her and she had told him she returned his love, but was it that easy? She was a possessive woman, she had discovered that. She knew now that she would not be able to settle for less than the whole of his heart, no matter what she'd told herself before.

He moved his lips to her ear and he hugged her. 'I can sense hesitation in you. You're not sure, are you?'

She wished she could say she were.

'Listen . . . ' He took her by her arms, gazing deeply into her eyes. 'I can't change the past. Women like Suzie have come into my life, but they meant nothing to me and never did I lead them to believe I was serious. In Suzie's case . . . I feel deeply sorry for her. But she has many male friends and I put her on that plane to one of them. Out of our lives, so that there were no more complications. So that I could work out my feelings for you.'

She gave a muffled sigh. 'And have you?'

He nodded, his grey eyes melting her. 'I knew from the first moment I talked to you; it was just admitting the truth to myself which was hard. I had to face the fact that I had stumbled across a woman who I was interested in, not just in the physical sense, but in other, deeper respects. You meet my every need, Tessa.'

Was it true? Did he really feel like that? There were so many beautiful, inviting women in his life. 'I know we work well together . . . ' she began, doubts tormenting her.

'It isn't just work. That's an added bonus, icing on my cake. Up until now part of my life has been in shadow. You were suddenly the sunshine. I was scared, damn it, hellishly scared. That was why I tried to put you out of my mind, hoping I wouldn't have to face the truth. I even sent you away.'

She frowned, astonished by the admission. 'The journalists . . . they were just an excuse?'

He nodded. 'I picked up that phone

at least twice a day while you were with your family. But I never got through dialling the whole of your number.'

'Oh, Sam . . . are you telling me the truth?'

He nodded. 'The absolute.' He put his lips to nuzzle her cheek. 'Nothing means anything in my life without you. Believe me, my darling.'

She hugged him, her hands closing over the body she adored. 'Kiss me, Sam.'

'Oh, my darling . . . I'll kiss you . . . a thousand times . . . '

His kiss and the caress of his hands made her glow with happiness. She would have to deal with her doubts, her insecurities by loving him all the more. And she could do it! She knew she could. She had come to know love was acceptance in all senses of the word, a tolerance of past and present and a belief in the future. This was the beginning of the future, whatever future they might have together. She was not asking for eternal commitment, strangely. Perhaps that was beyond hope. But Sam would be the only man in her life; she would have to pray she would be the only woman in his.

She pushed him gently away, her mouth lovingly bruised by his kisses. Smiling, trying to focus on the grey, glittering eyes which stared half-hooded down at her, she whispered, 'Do you think we had better make an effort to mingle with your guests?'

He nodded soberly. 'I want to dance with you. To feel your body moving against mine . . . knowing that you are mine.'

She slid her hands up into his hair. It was soft and thick. She coiled the strands around her fingers. 'I can't believe this is happening to us, Sam.'

'Believe it, my darling.'

It was not easy for her to leave the room. She felt as if walking through the doors might end the dream. But Sam pressed her closely to him, steering her through the clusters of people and on to the ballroom floor. The music was soft and sweet and very appropriate to their mood and he closed his arms around her, disclosing occasionally a few mutterings of love, as though they were in another world, unaware of the music or people. She gave herself up to the guidance of his arms, the slow, barely moving sway of their bodies, knowing people were staring and knowing that she didn't care.

What did it matter?

People would always stare at him. Perhaps he would always be a celebrity; he had that kind of charisma. Tenderly he held her, her eyes meeting his.

'Don't worry about the future, my darling,' he murmured gently.

'How can you read my thoughts?' she asked, smiling.

'You taught me how to do it. Remember that day in surgery, I told you I wasn't used to a double-act? It was bad of me to be so ruthless, but I was already beginning to love you and it wasn't a comfortable feeling. It was disturbing the foundations of my life.'

'I didn't mean to be intrusive. It was only a joke I made.'

'You scared the life out of me. No one ever understood what I was thinking . . . I wouldn't allow it. And then this little slip of a thing came along into my life, telling me how to mend drains . . . '

'Oh, Sam,' she laughed as he drew her closer, her skin tingling with aching desire, 'I would never have said that if I'd known who you were.'

He gave an amused groan. 'That was just the point. You didn't change your tactics at all. Even when you knew who I was, you very determinedly told me I couldn't judge a person's character in the time it takes to interview. Remember? You said a couple of weeks' trial was a far better idea.'

'I did, didn't I?' She blanched at her own temerity.

He kissed her, his lips warmly teasing. 'That's what I love about you. You're . . . you. The person I am holding in my arms is what I see with my eyes, is real. Not plastic or tinsel.'

She looked up at him, her green eyes rebuking. 'You told me everyone has a different side to them. You may have only seen the one side of me.'

'I'll take my chances and love both of them,' he mouthed. 'Equally.' He pulled her to him and a quiver of desire throbbed through her. She was frightened by her own passion, her overwhelming need of him. She didn't want to suffocate him and yet there was every chance of doing so. How long would their love last if she went out of control? This was always the question she had wrestled with in her life: how much control to keep. And it had been answered by the demands of her life at home. After losing a parent, someone you loved so much, there was always an element of doubt about the future. That was why she was so organised, as Sam saw it. It was a defence mechanism. With Sam, she had about as much organisation in her life as a mutineering crew on board a sinking ship. Her emotions were up in arms, her feelings in wonderful chaos, all centred on him, on her love for him. He told her not to worry about the future. But what was their future? she wondered, suddenly panic-stricken. She would have to love him unconditionally. Could she do it?

'May I have this dance. You can't monopolise her forever, old man,' Damien said, beside them.

'I'm going to have a damn good try,' Sam told him, smiling, but his voice had a warning note to it. She realised the music had stopped. Sam glanced down at her. 'Go and enjoy yourself, but come back to me.'

Damien held her lightly as the quartet struck up again. The lights dimmed and she saw Sam's head disappearing.

Now that he had disappeared from her arms and out of her sight she could hardly believe what had happened to her. Had Sam really told her he loved her? Had he kissed her like that, as if he never wanted to let her go?

Her feet seemed to guide her automatically. Damien talked, relieving her of the responsibility of making conversation, which was just as well because all her breath was taken away when she saw Sam emerge on to the floor with a tall, dark-haired girl.

He took her elegantly into his arms, the girl leaning into him like a willow into water. Tessa was transfixed; she couldn't move her eyes off them. The same old pain came back, just under her ribs, panic set in and she was feeling hot and slightly dizzy. Was tonight real at all? Was this crazy thing really happening to her? Now she knew what jealousy did to a person; just like grief, it distorted the perspective into an ugly, fragmented clone of truth.

Suddenly, across the room, Sam's eyes caught hers and she felt her body come back to life. That look was only for her. It restated all the wonderful things that he had said to her. It reaffirmed his love. She smiled back, their eyes locked until Damien whirled her the opposite way as the beat of the music began to quicken.

'We shall certainly miss this place,' Damien was saying, his wiry body doing gyrations in front of her to the rock beat.

She glanced up into his face. 'I'm sorry . . . what did you say, Damien?' The music was loud now.

'We were just getting used to this life of luxury,' he shouted. 'I'm going to miss Mrs Pearson's marvellous cooking.'

'Are you going somewhere?' she called, his arms tangling her in an intricate set of movements.

'Don't you know?' He stood still breathlessly, pulling down his jacket. 'The pilot is a no-go. Leo has given us the thumbs-down!'

Tessa shook her head. 'No, I had no idea. I'm sorry.'

Damien swept her into another fling.

'You'll miss us, will you?' he asked laughing.

Tessa grinned as she held on to his hand. 'A little, maybe.'

She was straining for breath when she escaped him, her body beginning to ache, her feet numb. She searched the room for Sam. He had disappeared. It was difficult to take in Damien's news. She was relieved to hear that life would soon be back to normal at Beechwood Bridge. But would life ever be normal again? The old doubts began to flood back. Sam had told her he loved her. But did he? If it were just an affair, if she had no say in their relationship, would she settle for that?

'I thought you were never coming off that floor.' Sam stood behind her as she whirled around. He was smiling, his eyes radiating a deep warmth which sent her heart into an immediate frenzy.

'I missed you,' she whispered and he pulled her to him.

'There are too many people here.'

She smiled. 'I only have eyes for one.'

'I want to make sure those green emeralds see no one else tonight. Let's walk.'

'You're crazy,' she laughed.

'Will you be warm enough in that?' His eyes flicked over her dress and her skin danced.

'It's a beautiful night outside, isn't it?'

'Come and see for yourself,' he teased. She allowed him to guide her through the couples, her heart racing. She could not turn back now. She had promised to love him unconditionally. This was the first moment of the beginning of their future together. When she stepped out of Beechwood Hall — and safety — she would step into an unknown world. Was she brave enough to embark on the journey? Sam had made no promises, suggested nothing except that he loved her. Could she return that love and expect only what he chose to give, freely, in return?

There was darkness all around. His arm slipped around her shoulders and she shivered, looking up at him. 'Come along, take this.' He removed his dinner-jacket, revealing a white shirt covering that broad chest. Her imagination ran riot, recalling the first time she had seen him unclothed, just wearing shorts, his skin as brown as a berry. As he draped the coat around her, he kissed her neck and the odour of his aftershave drifted sexily up into her nostrils. She took a breath. She was beginning to be drunk . . . and she had not even bothered to stop for a drink the whole evening. She was high on love.

Her hand slipped to the hard muscle at his waistline as they walked, every now and then, their thighs meeting in the darkness, the twist of his skin beneath her fingertips making her shudder convulsively.

'Where are you taking me?' she asked, her voice soft on the night air as they walked along the drive. 'Why do I have the feeling this is planned, Sam Wilde?'

He laughed gently, tipping up her

chin towards him, kissing the tip of her nose. In the darkness she tried to see his eyes. She felt them, even if she couldn't see them.

'Your woman's instinct is right. I am taking you somewhere.'

'And I'm trusting you enough to let you take me!'

'Which will be your downfall,' he whispered; 'into my arms.'

'I think I can just about bear to wait,' she laughed. She didn't care where they were going as long as she was with him. She would go wherever he wanted.

At the end of the drive, the horizon lay in darkness. To the right lay the road which wound through the village and out into the Forest. To the left lay the surgery, locked and asleep.

They arrived on the veranda.

It was dark, but the white wood shone out brilliantly, reflected in the moonlight. There were so many scents of flowers her head felt muzzy with them, like a tropical garden.

'Enter through here, all those who

dare,' he said, laughing softly, unlocking the door.

'Sam . . . ' She held him back. 'Tell me, why are the crew going? Are you going too? Are you leaving?'

She could see his shadow stiffen. 'Do you think I would leave you?'

'I . . . don't have any right to keep you to myself. I thought the filming meant a great deal to you.'

'My life has changed, my darling,' he whispered, taking her into his arms. 'I'm overjoyed Leo has taken that decision; it releases me to make plans for the future. A future for us, here in the Forest.'

'Don't say that just for me . . . ' She could barely speak.

'I want you to marry me, Tessa. To be my wife, to work with me, to live with me, to always love me. I won't permit anything to come between us. I won't take any risks with our love.'

'Sam . . . ' Her voice broke, tears sprang into her eyes. 'I can't let you make that commitment . . . '

'It's the only commitment I'm prepared to undertake,' he protested angrily, cupping her face between his hands. 'You have shown me trust. I want to honour that trust . . . always.'

'But marriage . . . ?' she gasped.

'I've waited a long time for this. I thought I would never achieve what I have over the last three months. No one is going to take that away from me.'

He pushed open the door and fingers of clematis fell from the bower above the porch, sweeping their fragrance over them like confetti. She walked in, dazed, unbelieving, her legs moving only because she told them to with a firm, silent command.

Sam switched on the light. The room was as it was always, except that now it was totally different. It was her future. She had loved it before, even when she first saw it, but now Sam loved it too. She knew deep down he had always loved this place.

He stood uneasily, a crooked smile playing at his lips. 'Will you marry me?'

'I love you, Sam,' she burst out, 'with all my heart. Yes, yes, a thousand times yes.'

He caught her in his arms, the taut pressure of his lean body accelerating her heartbeat. This kiss was very different. It held promise and intent to love . . . forever. There were no half-hearted measures in her life now. She knew where she stood with Sam Wilde, the man of her dreams and of reality.

Taking her by the hand, he led her into the recovery-room, a wide grin on his face. She stopped in the doorway, her jaw dropping. Two tiny golden heads bobbed out of a box inside a pen, sleepy eyes blinking a welcome against the sudden burst of light.

'Sam!' Tessa gasped. 'You haven't — '

'Tom has named them Primrose and Pansy. Poppy has gone to Jane and Ray at the Crossed Keys.' He bent down, picked up both wriggling puppies and, arms full, brought them to her. 'My gift of love . . . Mrs Wilde.'

They crowded into her arms, nibbling her chin and her nose, ferreting their way into her hair, and she laughed as Sam held her, the puppies between them.

'Oh . . . I'm going to cry,' she gasped, blinking. 'I'm so happy, darling.'

'Happy enough to take us on, all three, forever?'

She nodded, her eyes sparkling green gems, tinged with tears of happiness. 'Forever and ever and ever.'

THE END

We do hope that you have enjoyed reading this large print book.

Did you know that all of our titles are available for purchase?

We publish a wide range of high quality large print books including:
Romances, Mysteries, Classics
General Fiction
Non Fiction and Westerns

Special interest titles available in large print are:
The Little Oxford Dictionary
Music Book, Song Book
Hymn Book, Service Book

Also available from us courtesy of Oxford University Press:
Young Readers' Dictionary
(large print edition)
Young Readers' Thesaurus
(large print edition)

For further information or a free brochure, please contact us at:
Ulverscroft Large Print Books Ltd.,
The Green, Bradgate Road, Anstey,
Leicester, LE7 7FU, England.
Tel: (00 44) **0116 236 4325**
Fax: (00 44) **0116 234 0205**

AN UNEXPECTED ENCOUNTER

Fenella Miller

Miss Victoria Marsh has an unexpected encounter in the church with a handsome, but disagreeable, soldier who is recuperating from a grievous leg injury. Major Toby Highcliff believes himself to be a useless cripple, but meeting Victoria changes everything. Will he be able to keep her safe from the evil that stalks the neighbourhood and convince her he is the ideal man for her?

ANOTHER CHANCE

Rena George

School teacher Rowan Fairlie's life is
set to change when Clett Drum-
mond and his two young daughters
take on the tenancy of Ballinbrae
Farm. Clett insists he's come to the
Highlands to help the girls recover
from their mother's death, but
Rowan suspects there's more to it.
And why does her growing friendship with the family so infuriate the
new laird, Simon Fraser? Is it simple
jealousy — or are the two men
linked by some terrible mystery
from the past?

REBELLIOUS HEARTS

Susan Udy

Journalist Alice Jordan can't believe her misfortune when she literally bumps into entrepreneur Dominic Falconer. She is running a newspaper campaign to prevent him from destroying an ancient wood in his apparently never-ending pursuit of profit. However, when it becomes clear that local opinion is firmly on his side, Alice decides to go it alone. Someone has to stop him and she is more than ready for the battle. The trouble is — so is Dominic.

PASSAGE OF TIME

Janet Thomas

When charismatic Josh Stephens literally blows into her life, Melanie Treloar finds him a disturbing presence in the hostel she runs in west Cornwall. During his job of assessing some old mining remains Josh discovers a sea cave that holds an intriguing secret. When he is caught in a cliff fall — saving Melanie's niece — it is Melanie who comes to his rescue. Although this puts their relationship on a new level, can they solve the many problems that still remain?

ISLE OF INTRIGUE

Phyllis Mallett

Selina has come to Tarango to take up her inheritance — her father's sugar plantation — and she falls in love with the place from the moment of her arrival. There she meets the strikingly handsome Zack Halliday, who wants to buy her out, as does Hank Wayne, a tough American who won't take no for an answer. Then Fiona Stuart appears, wilful and jealous. Selina suspects the worst — and subsequent events prove her right . . .

da

N